Mirror to Mirror

RAJANI LaROCCA

Quill Tree Books
An Imprint of HarperCollinsPublishers

For Theresa, my "twin"

OVERTURE

Maya
She's the One

I don't like mirrors
but Chaya makes me look sometimes
at our twin reflections,
identical
almost.

The world sees
the same wavy black hair,
the same big brown eyes,
the same height,
the same voice,
but
Chaya's the one with
the brighter smile,
the quicker laugh,
the faster quip.
The world sees the goofball,
the talker,
the second.

But to me she's the one

who sees without showing
knows without telling
loves without asking.

She's the one.

Chaya
She's the One

People say they can't tell us apart, but that's ridiculous.
In the mirror, our identical faces are still different.
Maya's the one who shines and sparkles,
her eye keener, ear sharper, soul deeper.
Calm and composed her music floats,
soars above earth-bound notes.

The world sees (a) perfection(ist).

But to me,
she's the one I look up to, the one I come home to
the best part of me
in a separate space.

She's the one.

Maya
At the Edge

Summer sun sparkles on the lake.
I shiver on the mossy rock high above,
the sound of water and wind fading
as I look down
to the faces of friends
beckoning.
I can't hear their voices,
but I know they want me to
jump.
I want to,
but I'm stuck.
Their water-kissed smiles
call me
but still, I can't move.

I close my eyes,
frozen
until I feel a warm touch on my arm.
You don't have to jump, Chaya says, *but if you want to,
we can go together.*
Piercing through silence,

her voice is all the music
I'll ever need.
I nod
she takes my hand
Together

                                    we leap.

Chaya
Leap

Maya stares at the water.
I know she's conjuring all that might go wrong.
Sometimes she drowns
in possibilities.
You don't have to jump, I say, *but if you want to, we can go together.*
Sometimes you need to leap
and trust you'll land in the right place.
I take her hand, and together we jump
through the mirrored surface.
The water tugs us down,
but I pull up.

Part One
THE MIRROR

Chaya
Bet You

Bet you can't peel your orange in a single piece, I say.
                          Maya crinkles her nose with a
                          smile,
a smile that's exactly like mine,
just like the rest of her.
                        You're on, she says.
It's the week before school starts,
and we're in our backyard
with our little brother, Neel.

It's Gokulashtami, Lord Krishna's birthday,
so close to Neel's birthday
that I always think of it as his, too.
Mom has used a paste of rice flour and water
to make little footprints leading to the house,
like a divine toddler is visiting.
Maya and I wear matching salwar kameez,
                        Maya's blue
mine pink.
We've dressed Neel as Krishna
in a yellow kurta and dhoti,

his peacock-feathered crown flutters in the sun.
The day Neel was born, just over six years ago,
we were scared we might lose him,
but now the only way he disappears
is up a tree.

We distract Neel to keep him from climbing.
Last year, he ripped a hole in his outfit
five minutes after he'd gotten dressed.
But today, so far, it's working.

I inhale the citrus scent,
work my fingers under, through white pith,
stopping short of piercing soft flesh,
faster than Maya,
who approaches this challenge methodically,
like she does everything.

I'm almost done, the peel in a single piece,
when my hand slips   and it rips
with just a bit left on the orange.
I've lost the bet.

Maya's triumphant smile is like a perfect chord.
                    Did it! she says.
You win. I give her half my orange.

Maya Akka, Neel says.
Peel mine in one piece, too!

Our little brother is too much.
Too talkative, too adventurous,
too demanding, too loud.
But he's ours, and we love him.
The world can't tell us twins apart,
but Neel always knows who's who.
Maya peels the rest of the orange
in a single ragged piece.
Neel claps his hands.
You won twice! What do you get?

I know what I want—
for Maya not to worry, not to focus
on perfection,
to lose the shadows behind her eyes.

                Maya's smile crinkles her nose
                again.
                I want to share it all with you.

We eat the juicy fruit, licking sticky fingers
as a breeze stirs late August air
like a song.

Maya
Climbing

Dad jokes that Neel was born
under the sign of Lord Hanuman, the monkey god.
As a toddler, Neel climbed out of his crib to the top
of his bookcase. As a preschooler, he climbed the doorway of
his room, perched at the top like a mini-Spider-Man. He once
climbed so high in our maple tree that Mom nearly called the
fire department until Neel came down on his own, smiling
like he'd never stop. Now he understands
he needs to tell someone
where he's going,
and he can only
climb as high
as the swing set,
or he'll be
in trouble.
But sometimes
he forgets.
I shudder
to think
of him
forgetting,

climbing
too high
crashing
to
the
ground.

Chaya
The Art and Science of Dosas

Sunday mornings are for dosas.
Just like making music,
making dosas is both an art and a science
that Mom has perfected.

Mom's expert hands are always moving, sure and strong,
like Maya's on the piano.
She ladles dosa batter onto the cast-iron tawa
it hisses as she spreads it in a circle.
Bubbles burst on the surface of the pancake,
and when the bottom is golden brown
Mom puts it on a plate
and Maya spreads a spoon of coconut chutney—
creamy, chunky, just the right amount of spicy.
I scoop in potato and onion filling,
bright yellow from turmeric
soft, fluffy, sometimes crunchy from urad and chana dal
flecked with bright green kari leaves and cilantro.
Bet I can fold this without spilling, I say.
I spread the filling on half, fold the other half
over, watching Maya watch me.

I let a potato piece fall onto the plate
on purpose
because I want to show her
sometimes imperfect
is perfection.

Maya
Practice

I love Mom's pancakes
bursting with blueberries,
golden with apples.
And dosas are my favorite:
savory pancakes, crispy, spicy, fluffy, crunchy
flavors in perfect balance.

But whatever kind of pancake,
no matter how seasoned the griddle or tawa,
the first one never turns out right.
It sticks to the pan,
pale and limp and torn,
too small, too doughy.
Mom scrapes it off and says,
The first one is for practice,
the next one will be perfect.
She throws away the scraps
of useless pancake
no one will ever eat.

On the outside,

I'm just like my sister.
But on the inside, I'm
pale, doughy, useless,
stuck.
I'm the first one.
The one for practice.

Chaya
Music and Noise

Mom makes twin dosas for us twins.

> *Eat these while they're hot.*
>
> *You should eat, too,*
>
> Maya says.
>
> *We can make some for*
>
> *you.*

> *Soon,* Mom says.

But Mom doesn't leave the stove
until the kids have had two each
and Dad's had three.

> *Can we go to the park?* Neel asks.

Mom just started eating, I say.

> *It's all right, Chaya. Go have fun.*
>
> *I need to go grocery shopping.*

We'll wait for you, Dad says. *Then we'll all go to the park.*
He glances out the window. *A good kite-flying day. Or*
Rollerblading!

> *Both at the same time!* Neel squeals.

Yes! Let's clean up, says Dad. *Hurry!*

> Mom frowns as she takes
>
> another bite.

Maya and I clear the dishes as Neel bops
    around the kitchen like
        a tiny pinball.
Dad is a tornado,
grabbing silverware,
exclaiming at the hot pan handle,
dropping pots into the sink.
        Mom flinches with every clatter,
        every bang,
        eyes closed,
        jaw clenched.
There's an art and science to almost everything.
And what's music to Dad,
Mom finds a cacophony.

Maya
Major and Minor

Dad is a major chord
the funniest dentist
in the world—
boisterous,
joke-cracking, teasing.
When my patients laugh big,
they open their mouths wider, he says.
In the past, he used to go on adventures
with Keerthi Uncle,
but now he ropes us in instead.
Let's climb a mountain,
he might say
on a random Saturday. Or
Why haven't we been scuba diving yet?

Mom's a bank manager
who tells tellers what to do,
calms her clients
with her organized ways.
She plans our dinner menus,
posts them on the fridge.
Irons all our clothes,

even socks and underwear,
holds weekly inspections
of our rooms.
She turns to Dad
like a flower toward the sun,
but lately it seems
he's too loud, too wild,
too bright
to bear.
Mom's a melody that sighs
a minor chord
that brings tears
to your eyes.

Chaya
Bold

Be bold, says Dad.
Take up space. Don't be afraid.
You can do anything.
I hear his voice
when I'm faced with something scary:
a hard math problem
a mean classmate
a piano recital
a sudden thunderstorm.
But the scariest storm of all
is Maya's fear.
When she gets anxious, freezes like prey
stalked by some invisible predator,
that's when I grow bold.

Maya
Fear

Be careful is Mom's refrain.

Don't take anything with your left hand, she reminds us,
or the food may make you sick,
and you will fail at what you intend to do.

Mom says special prayers,
puts tiny dots of cooled incense ash
on the sides of our faces
to protect us from
the evil eye
that others may cast.

Superstitious nonsense, says Dad.
You're an educated woman.

Mom shakes her head.
There are things in the world
that can't be explained by logic.
She puts ash on our faces,
warns us against black cats,

tells us breaking a mirror
will lead to seven years'
bad luck.

Mom talks about
actions from past lives
having consequences today.
Her mom, our pati,
was sick for a long time,
struggled in her mind.
Her past lives must have caused it, says Mom.

That is scariest of all.
How can we make amends
for something we did
before we were born?
From lives
we can't remember?

Maya
Echo

The night before school starts
we've finished dinner and Neel asks,
Dad, can we play soccer?
Dad grabs him from his seat,
throws him over his shoulder.
Neel screeches with joy
and they race to put on shoes.
Running on full stomachs is not good for digestion, Mom calls.
But they're already out the door.
Mom sighs, brings plates to the sink,
starts scooping leftovers.
Chaya and I try to help.
Not that one, Maya.
Don't use the big container for beans.
Put the dal in there instead.
But I've already started.
Mom clicks her tongue,
takes it from me,
spoons the tiny bit of green beans
back into the serving bowl,
puts the barely used container

in the sink.

I'll take care of this. You two should get ready for school tomorrow.

We can help, Mom, I say.

Mom gives us a sad smile.

The biggest help would be

to get perfect grades this year for me.

She turns away.

I trudge upstairs

with *perfect*

ringing in my ears.

Chaya
The What If Game

Our room has twin windows, twin desks, twin beds.
Every night since we were little
as the dark house hums
we whisper *what-if*s to each other.
Once we used to dream of being warrior princesses
riding twin unicorns to our twin castles.
But now our discussions are different.

> *What if this year's too*
> *hard?* Maya asks.

What if it's even better? I counter.

> *What if music gets too*
> *complicated?*

What if we play the most beautiful pieces ever?

> *What if you're*
> *my favorite sister?*

What if you're mine?

Chaya
First Day

of seventh grade.
We don't wear the same clothes anymore,
but our clothes, like us, are related.

Maya likes dark jeans,

I like light ones, ripped at the knees.

She likes a plain tee,

I like stripes.

She puts her hair in a
bouncy high pony,

I like mine down,
swishing around my shoulders.
We're identical

but Maya's more
thoughtful
more intense.

I'm just a little dull

compared to her
brilliance.

I'm the one who tries
to fill her silences with chatter,
tries

to make her shake with laughter.

First day of seventh grade.
It's going to be a good year.
I promise.

Maya
Homeroom

Chaya and I get off the bus
stop by our lockers
go to separate homerooms
on the first day of our second year
at Atherton Middle.

My breath hitches as I walk down the hall.
I miss the summer—
playing music in the sweet Maine air
of Camp Allegro,
toasting marshmallows,
swimming in the lake.
We're back to reading and writing and science and math
and grades.
School will be all right. Better than all right. Fun, Chaya says.
Everything's fun to her.
But now that I'm home, we're home
the fear rises in me
like a cold wave
of silence.
One more year, I remind myself.

One more year of ~~being~~
trying to be
perfect.
One more year
and I'll be free, we'll be free,
finally.

I walk into homeroom,
give Jay a wave
smile at his grin.
At least he's here.

But though we haven't shared homeroom
for years,
it still doesn't feel like home
without Chaya.

Chaya
Anisa

Hello, Charming, says Anisa.

        Hi, Anazing, I reply.

Anisa's like the oboe she plays in wind ensemble:
soft and mellow, with occasional
squeaks.
She likes everything from orchestra to pit band,
electric guitar and radio sing-alongs.
This summer at Camp Allegro, she even landed a small part
in the musical.
Wish I'd tried out, too. But Maya didn't want to.

Anisa's grin is a beam of light (even before she got braces).
We've shared homeroom and classes together
ever since Maya and I were forced apart way back in fourth
grade.
We compare schedules. All the same but math and English!
Chool! she says.

        Anstounding, I reply.

It's good to be back.

Maya
Jay

Jay's saved me a seat in homeroom,
an island of calm in the chaos.
My classmates are
s t r e t c h e d - o u t versions
of their sixth-grade selves,
tan and relaxed,
catching up on summer adventures,
looking forward to the year ahead.

We've known Jay for as long as
we've been alive.
What were the chances that Dad and his best friend
would both have children
on the same day?
Triplets, our parents joke
though Chaya always reminds me
we have a *real* brother.
Chaya thinks Jay's full of hot air,
the same air he blows through his trumpet.

But I see
the cold kiss of sadness
underneath.

Chaya
Life Science

is what we're studying this year.
In other words: biology.
Anisa and I pass notes
as Mr. Selvig goes over what we'll cover:
Cells
We're more complicated than amoebas,
I write.

**Classifications of
living things**
*We're classified as
awesome*, Anisa writes.

Genetics
I pause.
*How can two people have the exact same genes,
but be so different inside?*
I put my pen down.
I don't have the heart to write it.

Maya
Poetry

I'm with Chaya
for Language Arts
where we're told our first unit
is poetry.
This will be a journey of self-discovery, says Ms. Meyer.
We'll be reading poetry
and writing it, too.
Chaya grins, and I know
she's thinking of song lyrics,
rhymes,
rhythm.
I prefer music
to words.
Music can go places
words can't reach.

Chaya
Extra

Maya and I come to lunch together, but Jay squeezes in line
between us.

    Hey Maya, want to come over tomorrow after school?
We have piano, I reply.

> *Maybe Thursday?* Maya
> asks.

    I've got cross country, says Jay. *What about—*
Let's get lunch first, I say. *I'm starving.*

> Maya nods, moves up
> in line.

    I've got my lunch packed, says Jay.
Then you can run and get a table, I tell him.

> Maya raises her
> eyebrows.

    But Jay turns away and finds us seats
in the seventh-grade section, open to us now.
Didn't you just have class with him? I ask.

> *He wants to hang out*
> *with us.*

He only asked you.

Maybe you could try a
little harder?

Maybe, I say. But I won't.
 Jay's always there,
 at school, at camp,
 at home,
 the extra note
 that mars our perfect interval.

Maya
Lessons

Piano lessons are my favorite part of the week.
Our teacher, Mrs. Yusofsky, is a kindred spirit.
She demands the best of all her students,
from posture: *back straight*
> *elbows in*
>> *wrists level*

to technique: *hammer fingers*
> *strength from the core*
>> *pinch the staccato*

to musicality: *move with the rhythm*
> *live the dynamics*
>> *feel the music*

I love Mrs. Yu's Russian accent, strong fingers, flawless playing.
During my lessons, I forget everything else:
homework and tests,
worry and regret,
and just get lost
in the music.

Today, at our first lesson of the school year,
Chaya and I are together.

We tell Mrs. Yu about the music at camp
and she plays samples of Chopin, Bach, Mozart,
asks us what we'd like to work on.
Chaya and I don't need to discuss.
We share a look

Bach

we say in unison.
Chaya and I
perfectly in sync.

Chaya
Better

Bet we can go faster, I say.
It's a Saturday in September.
Maya and I take turns at the piano
while Neel draws pictures nearby.
Bach's Invention no. 4 is fast and dramatic,
right hand melody picked up by the left,
point and counterpoint,
back and forth back and forth back and forth
tension building   building   building
building   to the end.
Maya plays the piece three times, faster with each repetition,
rhythm unwavering as a metronome.
Then I take a turn—not as precise, but full of energy.
Like most bets with my sister,
I don't want to win, just to dare her
into a small adventure.

Maya-Chaya, someone says in the kitchen.
As the older one by five minutes, Maya's always first,
even though I'm first alphabetically.
Keep playing, I signal, mime getting a glass of water.

I peek into the kitchen,

where Mom's having tea with Vimala Auntie—

Jay's mom,

who has a face full of makeup and flaunting opinions.

Auntie, we call her, but she's not Mom's sister, not anyone's

sister.

Which one is playing now? Auntie asks.

I have no idea, says Mom.

Behind me, Maya's fingers fly, pulling sound.

Which one is better? Auntie asks.

Mom pauses. I hold my breath.

They're both excellent.

But one must be better, Auntie says.

She takes a sip of tea,

clinks her cup in the saucer.

You should focus

on developing that one's musical talent.

The other can do something else.

They must be distinct to get into top colleges.

My Arvind . . .

Of course. Perfect Arvind at Princeton.

Does she give advice to her other son, Jay,

the "triplet" we never wanted?

To me, Jay's just like his mother—

all show, no substance.

>> *They are twelve years old,*
>> Mom says.
>> *We don't need to worry*
>> *about college yet.*

It is never too early to start worrying, Auntie says.
You never know what sudden changes life can bring.
It's true. We all miss her husband, Keerthi Uncle.
Sadly, we're still stuck with her.

>> *Hi, Vimala Auntie.*
>> I head straight for the sink, take two glasses,
>> turn on the tap.

Hello, Maya.   >> I don't bother to correct her.
>> *You know, each of us*
>> *is better at different things on piano.*

Oh?

>> *My sister's better at the right hand,*
>> *and I'm better at the left.*

Ah.

>> *We'd get arm transplants,*
>> *but we can't decide who'd get the best.*
>>> *Chaya!* Mom scolds. *Don't be*
>>> *ridiculous!*
>> But I can see she wants to laugh.

Auntie purses her lips.

Bye, Auntie. I bow my head, leave with
the water
hide my smile until I cross the
threshold.

Maya
Notes Inégales

My hands try to match
all the music in my mind
but they never do.

I'm reaching for that
flawless sound, faultless rhythm
that lives inside me.

I wish I could learn
to love the striving, not fret
about the playing.

I wait for the day
the music in my mind
comes out right.

Chaya
Matched Set

Maya stumbles just before the end of the piece.
She stops, starts again. Her trill's not fast enough.
She stops, thumps the keys.
A storm's coming on like an ache in my bones. But sometimes
I can stave it off.
Let's play our song. Together, I say.

                                        Maya nods.

We scoot so our thighs touch.
I play the left hand   she plays the right
we move between staccato and legato
the melody shifting between us   like tossing a ball.

It's "Matched Set," our favorite song from the musical
Long Lost,
the story of twin girls separated at birth
who become pen pals through school,
then meet at summer camp.
Maya and I grew up singing this song,
it's what we hum as we fall asleep.
A song about twin sisters, unknown and incomplete
without each other.

A song about finding your other half.
We're a matched set, Maya and I,
and nothing will ever separate us.
We sing: *All our lives, we've been wandering,*

> *and now we're finally*
> *home.*

Maya didn't hear Auntie's poison about which of us is better.
But what if Mom listens, makes one of us give up piano?
I'll never let that happen.

Neel taps me on the shoulder.
The green crayon broke off in my ear, he says.
Maya and I leap to our feet
the bench scrapes against the floor with a groan.

> Maya asks, *Does it hurt?*
> *Can you hear?*

Just feels funny, says Neel, jiggling with his finger.
Why'd you stick a crayon in your ear? I ask.
Don't know, he says.

> *Come on*, Maya says.
> *We need Mom.*

I give Neel a piggyback ride into the kitchen.

Maya

C

Mom says we don't need
to come to the doctor,
but I need to.
Chaya comes, too, though
I can tell she's more worried about me
than Neel.
Waiting
reminds me of the waiting   we did all those years ago
when Neel was born.
Cold silence descends,
numbing ice that spreads,
and the world blurs.
I turn away from Chaya,
press my thumbnail
into the soft flesh
of my palm
just to feel
something.
It makes a C that fades in a moment.
But my guilt, my worry
can't fade.

I must be careful
to keep those I love
from harm.
I press a C into the soft flesh
of my palm
again
again
a sting that stays

even after Mom and Neel emerge,
and he is smiling,
he is fine.

Chaya
What-Ifs

That night at bedtime:
What if Neel got super-hearing from that bit of crayon in his ear?
I ask.

> *What if his hearing's damaged?*
> says Maya.

What if you're worrying too much?

> *What if I should have watched him*
> *more closely?*

What if you're not playing this game right?

> Maya sighs. *What if . . . his*
> *superpower is floating?*

Yes! What if whenever Neel climbs up from now on,
he never has to climb down, but floats down instead?

> *What if he touches us,*
> *and we can float, too?*

What if while we float, music floats around us?

> Maya grins. *What if it's*
> *"Matched Set"?*

What if you're my favorite sister?

> *What if you're mine?*

We hum "Matched Set" and drift into sleep.

Chaya
Silence

lives in our home in many ways.
Silence between notes and phrases, the pauses   that give
music meaning.
Silence between sisters, closer than sisters,
who understand without words.

But then there is
Silence   when Maya looks stricken
Silence   when she starts to shake
Silence   when I ask what's wrong
Silence   in Mom's expectations
                                           in Dad's clenched jaw
                                           in Maya's frozen face
Silence   that's unnatural
                                           heavy
There are two kinds of silence:
one that's open

                                           one that's secret.

Maya
Twins Who Fly

Chaya and I watch Neel
as he climbs the red maple in our back yard.
October makes the leaves
a bold crimson.
The world is filled with music:
birdsong,
breeze,
the Earth itself,
changing.
I pick a twin seedpod
hanging from a low branch,
the outside brown and rough,
the inside full of possibility.
I toss it in the air.
What if, it says as it flutters to earth
What if
What if
What if
Our parents say the seeds
remind them of us:
Chaya and I,

twins who fly, who dance
to the music around us,
make music of our own.
They hope we fly far and wide
before coming down
to take root and flourish.

But I feel my wings were clipped
years ago.
Instead of flying,
I crashed
and threaten to do the same
to all I love.
My *what-if*s are full
of fear.
Chaya and I
not quite
a matched set.

Chaya
Shy

For the first few years we knew Anisa,
she barely spoke.
And when she did, it was a whisper so soft
it barely registered
as speaking.
In third grade,
we all started the recorder in school.
While most kids played those plastic flutes
like instruments of aural torture,
Anisa played it like she cared.
You can read music? she asked us,
wide-eyed and thrilled.
So we asked her over one afternoon,
taught her all we knew.
When Mrs. Turner came to pick Anisa up,
we played a concert for her and Mom:
a round of "Frère Jacques" on three recorders.
How about that, said Anisa's mom.
Anisa's so good. And she wants to play the clarinet, I declared
as Anisa hid behind me, too shy
to ask for anything

since her parents split up
and money was tight.
But I had no problem
asking.
And that's how we became
best friends.
(Other than Maya, of course.)
The next week, Anisa got a clarinet,
and year by year,
her shyness melted a little more.
In sixth grade, Anisa moved to oboe,
which is even cooler
than clarinet.
She's still soft-spoken,
but her music
speaks volumes.
And she never has trouble
speaking to me.

Chaya
Wind Ensemble

Anisa and I hurry to the music room
that smells of old carpet, musty paper, sweat,
and sounds of aimless student chatter, random notes.
Anisa starts us off on oboe and everyone tunes to her,
tries to blend.
Except one person:
Jay
playing arpeggios on his trumpet,
bending notes,
winning the award for Most Annoying Person.
I scowl and turn to Maya
but she's smiling. Ugh.
Rao, cut it out, calls Mr. Gilsdorf, our teacher.
Jay stops until Mr. G is distracted, then starts up again, more
softly.
A jazzy riff
that sounds smoky, like the bonfire at camp.
Show-off.
Mr. G goes over what we'll be playing
for our first semester concert.
The eighth-grade pianists from last year have moved on,

so that leaves Maya and me free to switch
back and forth on piano for every piece.
Five songs, five chances for us to play.

We get our schedules and music, and it's already time to go.
How will you decide who gets to play what?
Jay asks smugly.
Go away, Jay, I say.
Maya has enough stress without feeling
like I'm competition.
We'll figure it out at home, I tell Maya.

       She nods.
The bell rings. Jay tugs at Maya's sleeve.
We need to move it to get to Spanish on time—

       and she lets herself be pulled
       out the door.

With Jay. Without me.
And suddenly I miss her
like she's going further than just the other end of school.
Chome on, says Anisa. *Ready for science?*
Ansolutely, I say, not feeling ready at all.

Maya
Almost a Brother

Jay is almost our brother.
Born on the same day,
we grew up together.
First bike rides,
hide-and-seek with neighborhood kids,
beach and mini golf on Cape Cod.
Knock-knock jokes,
talks late into the night
huddled in a blanket fort.
Then Keerthi Uncle died,
and everything changed.

I know the way Jay acts
is cover for the hurt inside.
How come Chaya, who's so good to me,
when it comes to Jay,
loses all her generosity?

Chaya
Identical

I look up twins for science class.
If an embryo splits into two within the first week,
they become identical twins, like Maya and me.
If the split happens between days 8 and 12,
they are mirror twins, mirror images
of each other, often left- and right-handed,
And if twins split after that—day 13 or later,
they are conjoined,
physically connected, forever.

I stroke the tiny birthmark on my left wrist
that Maya doesn't have.
Maya and I have the same DNA
almost.
We started off identical,
but each time a cell divides,
it can change.
And as a person grows,
their DNA changes even more.
So, science supports what I already know:
that Maya and I, who started the same,

grow more different with every breath.

I want to return to that time
when we were the same
to that time
before her sadness began.

Maya
Dissonance

We're six,
at the mall with Mom and Dad,
buying supplies for the baby
due in two months.
And the checkout line is
so
so
so
l o n g.

While Mom waits in one line,
while Dad waits in another,
Chaya and I play hide-and-seek
among the racks of clothes.
Bet you can't find me, she says.
The catch:
we need to spot each other in Mom's mirror.
Be careful, Mom says as she hands it to me.
She's already told us
breaking a mirror causes
seven years' bad luck.

The plastic compact
looks like a circle,
but when open,
it's double circles,
one mirror for Chaya,
one for me,
like a pair of shining eyes.

Chaya and I dance around the racks of dresses,
tables piled with sweaters and T-shirts,
tall end caps with pants and shorts.
We tiptoe on the tiled floor,
careful not to step on cracks.
The one who is It
holds the mirror,
tries to angle it to catch the other.
It's fun to try to escape the mirror,
to squat or lie or stand
in plain sight.
The game is in the seeking,
not the finding.

But then I'm It
and I can't find Chaya,
no matter how I try.
There are two mirrors,

and she's not in either one.
Until at last, I hear a giggle nearby,
but I see no reflection.

I spin to look,
my arm outstretched,
and hear a crack,
for I've smacked
the open compact
against the sharp edge of a shelf.
One circle has a jagged fracture
running right down the center,
like a bolt of lightning,
a hideous flaw that splits my face in two,
the eyes now misaligned,
dissonant.
I reach my finger and trace it,
pull my hand back in pain,
a drop of blood welling.
I drop the compact under a rack of clothes
as if leaving it there means
I'm not guilty.

Mom, her arms full of bags,
finally finds me.
Where is Chaya? she asks.

I look across the aisle and see
my sister giggling with Dad
as he shows her cuddly toys for the baby.

I hold up my finger,
and Mom gasps,
Maya! What happened?
I can't answer.
She clutches her big belly.
Come. Let's get you cleaned up.

Mom leads me to the bathroom
and washes my hands,
makes sure the bleeding has stopped,
asks me again what happened.

My tears fall silently,
not for my stinging finger,
but for the perfect mirror,
a thing of beauty,
now ruined.
I'm terrified,
can't tell her the truth
because what if that makes
the bad luck start?

We leave the mall
Mom asks for the mirror
and I say I lost it.
I told you to be careful, she says with a frown.
When Chaya asks me what's wrong,
I say my finger hurts,
worried
if I tell her about it,
she'll be part of the bad luck, too.

For the first time in my life,
I keep a secret from my sister.
The next day,
the bad luck starts.
For that is when
our brother is born,
much too early.
And it's all my fault.

Chaya
Storm

Thunder wakes me on the night Neel is born.
I sit up in the dark,
call for Maya,
who comes to my bed and holds me.
With the next flash of lightning,
we run to our parents' room
to find them gone.
Downstairs, Vimala Auntie sits in the kitchen
drinking tea.
Where are Mom and Dad? I ask.

At the hospital, says Auntie.

The baby's coming.

I feel Maya stiffen beside me.
It's not time yet, I say. *Will the baby be okay?*
Vimala Auntie pats our heads, asks if we want hot chocolate.

Sometimes silence
is a kind of lie.

Maya
Almost

Our baby brother lives.
But because of the bad luck I caused,
he almost did not.

Chaya
Blue

Why so blue?
says a character in a cartoon Neel's watching.
He asks us what that means.
Blue means sad, I say.
Why? Neel asks. *It's not a sad color. It's my name, right?*
You're right, I say. *Your name means blue.*
It's Krishna's color, a happy color.
Neel isn't satisfied.
Do you know why, Maya Akka?

No, says Maya, looking
at the ground.

Why so blue? I ask without speaking.
But she doesn't answer.

Maya
Repeat

Seven years is a long,
long
time
to pay for breaking
such a small thing.
But in the hollows
of the years that follow,
bad luck comes,
and, like a section in a piece of music,
it repeats.
Not just for me, but for those I love.

When we're seven,
Mom's purse is snatched
before our eyes,
the thief running like a blur
on the boardwalk
under summer stars.

When we're eight,
Dad's car is struck

by a tractor trailer skidding on ice.
The car is crushed like a can.
Dad's lucky to escape
with just a broken leg.

When we're nine,
we go to Camp Allegro,
our sleepaway music camp,
for the first time.
We love making music
in the green woods of Maine,
adding our notes to those of the birds' and insects' songs.
I forget about bad luck until the last day,
the day our parents come to watch us perform,
when I trip on a root running from my cabin
to the concert hall,
land on my face,
break a tooth,
bleed all over my dress.

Bad luck pursues me,
year by year.
Seven years is a long,
long
time.

Chaya
What's in a Name?

In English we're asked to write poems about our names,
what they mean to our families, to us.
My parents always told me *Chaya* means
living, luster, beauty.
But when I search, I come across a different meaning,
one from a Hindu myth:

> *The goddess Sanjna was the wife of the sun god, Surya.*
> *After giving him three children, she could no longer bear*
> *Surya's brightness.*
> *She abandoned her husband and children,*
> *and left her shadow, Chaya,*
> *whom she fashioned to look exactly like herself,*
> *to be the sun god's wife in her place.*
> *And Chaya, the ever-dutiful shadow,*
> *took Sanjna's place and pretended to be Lord Surya's wife.*

I take a breath, read again.
My name means *dark reflection, shadow.*
And I guess I am Maya's shadow,
following wherever she goes.

                                        She's the bright one

I'm right beside her

> when she's in the
>
> spotlight.

I turn in a piece about my name meaning *luster*.

But I also write a poem just for me,

one that no one else will read:

> *I was born after.*
>
> *I'm the bonus,*
>
> *the extra,*
>
> *my name chosen for rhythm,*
>
> *for rhyme,*
>
> *whatever was needed*
>
> *to round out the stanza,*
>
> *complete the song.*
>
> *I'm the shadow*
>
> *of the one who*
>
> *shines.*

I love Maya more than anyone.

Just like Chaya from the myth,

I'll do anything to make her happy.

Maya
In the Mirror

In the mirror,
we look identical.
But the mirror can't show everything.

Maya means *dream*,
a dream
that God can give us,
a dream
that we keep striving toward.

Maya also means *illusion*,
the illusion
God can cast over us,
to make us believe
what isn't real.

I try to live up to the dream
but what if I'm just
the illusion?

Chaya
Irritation

Besides Jay, the runner-up for Most Annoying Person
is Abby,
the princess with ironed hair, designer clothes, competitive
ways.

    What'd you get for number six on the homework?
    she asks Maya after math class.

                Um, says Maya, *let me
                think.*

She got the right answer, I say.
    Abby smirks at me.
    I asked Maya.
    You're so alike, but also not.
Why do you care? I ask.
    Just curious, Abby says.

                Twelve, says Maya.
                That's what I got.

    Oh, says Abby.

                What about you? asks
                Maya.

Abby just walks away.

It's just two points, I say to her retreating back.
You'll make them up somehow, I'm sure.

Maya
Wrong

We're studying for a math test
and I should get everything right.
I press my nail into my palm:
C C C C C C
Let's take a break, Chaya says.

> *Just three more problems.*
> I finish writing,
> look at the answers
> in the back of the textbook,
> bite the soft skin around
> a fingernail.
> *I got half a problem wrong*, I say.

Chaya peeks over my shoulder.
Just an arithmetic mistake.

> *I can't make stupid errors like this.*
> The room starts to blur.

Let's stop for tonight.

> *No, I can't stop*
> *until I get them all right!*

I should be able
to get them all right.

Chaya
Ozone

There's ozone in the air—
soon, lightning will flash.
Then I get an idea.
Bet I can write the words to "Long Lost"
faster than you, I say.

       Maya looks up and blinks. *What?*
I know that song better than anyone.
Even you, I say.

       Her eyes narrow. *Are we writing or typing?*
And just like that, the dumb math problem
is forgotten.
We take out our notebooks and pens,
and I set the stopwatch on my phone.
Go!

       Finished! Maya says.
I stop the timer. I'm two words away
from done.
Let's see. I pretend to be skeptical.
 All my life,
 I've been wondering why the world seeks to defeat me.

All my life,
I've been searching for the one who completes me.
She's gotten every word right, of course. And at the end:
All my life, I've been wondering why I felt so alone,
And now I've found you,
and I'm finally home.
We sing the last stanza together
like there's only one voice between us.
The song fades away
and Maya finally looks me in the eye. *Thank you.*
I rest my forehead against hers.
You need to talk to Mom and Dad.

She looks away.

You need help. There's only so much
I can do.
You need help. Not just from them.
Maybe from a professional.

She shakes her head,
eyes round.
Remember how Vimala Auntie gossiped
about that girl from the temple
with acne?
Can you imagine what she'd say
if it got out that I'm crazy?
You're not crazy. You just need help.
And who cares what Vimala Auntie says?

She shakes her head again.
You're all the help I need.

I hug her. I'll always help.
But what will happen
when I can't be with her?

Neel bursts into the room.
Can we climb the maple in the dark?
No, I say. *Remember the rules.*
Also, it's freezing out there.

But we can make the best
pillow fort ever, says Maya.

And we do.

Maya
Variations on a Theme

If I can think of all the bad things
that could happen,
maybe
they won't.
I'm constantly aware
of danger in the air.

But I soon understand
there's more badness in the world
than I can think of.
So I decide
the way to combat bad luck
is to be perfect.
That if I can be perfect,
I can overcome the imperfect
things that happen.
But it's exhausting,
all-consuming,
to forever worry
about what bad thing
is coming next

to forever try to be flawless
to make up for
my biggest flaw.

I dig my nail into my palm
to remind me.

Chaya
Forty

Mom's turning forty, and we have a party
to celebrate with our closest family friends.
Somehow, she loves spending days cooking and cleaning
for her own birthday.
Half an hour before guests are due,
the food is done, the house sparkling,
and we're all dressed up and ready—
Come open your presents, Dad says.

> *After the party*, says Mom.

*You'll spend too much time cleaning,
and then you'll be too tired*, Dad says.

> *I don't need anything.*

Too late. Dad's grin is as wide as his arm span.

  Everyone needs presents on their birthday, Neel says.
We coax her into the living room, arrange the gifts
on the coffee table.
Neel gives Mom a tiny model of the Eiffel Tower,
painted in a rainbow of colors.

  I want to climb to the top with you someday, Mommy.

> *Yes, putta*, Mom says, crinkling
> her nose

and rubbing it against his.
I'll climb it with you,
just like I did with Daddy.
But you must promise
you'll use the stairs.

Neel giggles, snuggles against her.

Mom glances at the clock.
Twenty minutes before our
guests arrive.
Vimala Auntie might even be
early.

Maya and I hand Mom a tiny box.
It's wrapped too tightly to save the paper,
so she's forced to rip it.
I grin   Maya winces.
Inside is a small purple piece of plastic.

A thumb drive? Mom asks.

I nod. *Forty songs for your fortieth birthday,*
of Maya and me playing your favorite pieces.

We'll help you get them on your
phone, Maya says.

Somehow we've managed to surprise her.

Oh girls, Mom says.
I couldn't ask for a better present.

She envelops us,
one squeezed in each arm,

and I inhale the smell of cumin from cooking
and her special Mom scent of roses and vanilla.
My turn, Dad says, sliding a large square box over.

> *Our guests will be here soon,*
> Mom says.
> *We should wait.*

They'll be here all night, Dad says. *Come on, live a little.*
He waggles his eyebrows.
Open it, Nalini, my flower.

> Mom laughs
> like she can't help it.

Maya
Surprise

The top of the box is wrapped separately from the bottom.
Mom lifts the lid
and gold and silver confetti stars explode
over her sari, her hair,
the table, the sofa, the floor—
our perfect room,
covered in chaos.
Surprise! Dad says.
He tries to hand her an envelope from the box.

                                    Mom doesn't take it.

Dad fans out glossy brochures
to show us all.
We're going back to Paris next summer! All of us!
   We're going to Paris? Neel leaps off the sofa,
   rolls on the floor
   like a happy puppy.
Mais oui, mon frère, Dad says in an atrocious French accent.
*Mommy and I haven't been there since our honeymoon
a hundred years ago.* He smiles at Mom, squeezes her stiff hand.

                              Mom blinks, gives him a half-
                              smile back.

Next summer? I ask.

But Chaya and I will be at camp.

I know, kanna, Dad pats our shoulders.

We're going after camp. Don't worry,

nothing will interfere with my girls' summer of music.

PARIS! Neel yells.

He dances around the coffee table,

tossing sparkly confetti like a flower girl.

Daddy! I want to climb the Eiffel Tower in our yard

NOW!

You got it, little man! Dad hoists Neel on his shoulders,

and they pretend to be a two-headed monster as they go out

the sliding door.

I glance at the sparkles on my hand—

tiny stars, birthday cakes, "40" in gold and silver

jubilant

but not to Mom.

Her face droops

as she stares at the chaos around us.

The doorbell rings.

Chaya
Leap

I leap
into action.
Get cleaned up, Mom.
We've got this.

> Mom's eyes spill over. *Thank you, girls.*
> She unpins her hair, shakes it out,
> and sparkles float down
> as she goes upstairs.

I sweep confetti off the table,
pick up discarded wrapping paper.
It's got to be Vimala Auntie, I say to Maya.
Bring her to the kitchen and distract her.
I'll take care of this room.

> I get the vacuum
> as Dad and Neel
> laugh in the yard.

Maya
Tremolo

Vimala Auntie and Jay
are at the mudroom door.
They never use the front door anymore,
not since Keerthi Uncle died.
We miss his hearty laugh, his terrible jokes,
his solid presence at concerts,
nodding along in the front row.
Dad misses him most of all,
his partner in business and adventure.
They used to go
kayaking under a full moon
skydiving on their birthdays
race car driving for no reason at all.

Since Uncle's heart suddenly gave out,
Vimala Auntie has puffed up like a poori,
too hot for bare fingers,
with a paper-thin skin the slightest touch can rupture.
I put on a smile, wave them inside,
ask them to sit for a moment
while I bring drinks and snacks.

Where is Mummy? Vimala Auntie asks, roving an eagle eye
over the spotless kitchen
but there's nothing here to criticize.
I take a nice glass,
pour her favorite orange soda,
hear the ice crack.
She's just finishing her hair, I say.
As I hand Auntie her glass, I notice
a golden birthday cake confetti piece on my hand.
My hand shakes, soda sloshes.
Chaya, watch, says Auntie,
clucking her tongue,
moving her silk sari away from the spill.
I don't bother to correct her,
set the glass down in a hurry,
rush to grab a paper towel.
But Jay has already brought a bunch.
I got it, he says, squatting down and mopping up the small spill.
Hey, Maya, he murmurs under his breath.
We straighten up and I can't help but smile
for real, this time.

Chaya
After

a night full of laughter
with so many friends,
music and toasts to Mom,
and a raucous rendition of "Happy Birthday."
After the many well wishes,
thoughtful presents,
feasting and laughter,
there's tension trembling underneath.
After our guests have gone
to their happy homes
and we've cleaned up
our messy one.
After all that,
we return to our normal state of late:
Neel sleeping,
Mom weeping,
Dad fuming,
Maya brooding,
me fretting.
Because even a celebration
causes conflict.

Maya
Concert

The wind ensemble concert is two weeks before
winter break.
And I'm supposed to play piano for three of five pieces,
Chaya two.
Neither of us has a starring role,
but we want to do well.
In the weeks before the concert,
I'm overwhelmed
with numbing silence.
I press my thumbnail
C C C C C C
into the flesh of my left hand
over and over.
The week before the concert
my hand hurts too much to reach for octaves.

So that night, I ask Chaya   *What if you played the Williams piece?*
Why?

     What if I said you're not playing
     the What If game right?
She huffs. *What if I asked you why?*

     What if I've heard you practice

and know you'd be fantastic?

What if I'm worried about you?

What if I'm fine?

What if I don't believe you?

What if you're incredible
and should get your chance to shine?

Pause.

What if you're my favorite sister?

What if you're mine?

We clear our switch with Mr. G,
and at the concert,
Chaya is her brilliant self.

But I still can't stop worrying
can't stop pressing *what-if*s
into my hand.

Chaya
Clumsy

One week before our piano recital with Mrs. Yu,
and Maya's hands aren't moving like they should.
Her left hand isn't nimble, doesn't fly across the keys
like usual.
Every time she stumbles,
I hold my breath, waiting
for the lightning strike.
But Maya doesn't quake with silent tears.
She keeps going and winces.
What's wrong? I ask.

> She shakes her head,
> makes a fist,
> hides it.

I gently take her hand
and find it's bleeding.

Chaya
Itch

Maya's hand is raw,
covered in tiny cuts
that look like *Cs*.
How long's it been like this? I ask.

> She looks away. *A few days.*

Maya, I say.

> *Fine. A few weeks. Maybe months.*

Does it hurt?

> She shakes her head. *More like an
> itch.*

Why didn't you tell me?

> *We've been busy.*

This is bad. You're bleeding!
We have to tell Mom.

> *She's got enough to worry about.*

But I'm done asking.
I take Maya's hand, the one that doesn't hurt,
and bring her to Mom.

We go to the doctor, who prescribes a cream.
No more scratching, she says.

The next week at the recital,
Maya plays Bach's Invention no. 8
and her hands fly.
But I can't shake the feeling
that Maya hasn't told me all the truth.
It's like an itch
I just can't reach.

Maya
Perfect

Chaya plays Bach with less precision,
but more force,
more emotion
than me.
She projects the confidence
I wish I had.
Her Invention no. 4
is dramatic
the way it's supposed to be.
I don't pay attention to whether
she misses notes,
because her playing is so lovely,
it doesn't matter if it's not
technically perfect.
It's perfect.
She's perfect
to me.

Chaya
Up Here

It's winter break
and Maya's stopped fiddling with her hand.
For a few days, we go to Vermont to ski—
Mom's not enthusiastic,
but the rest of us are excited enough
to make up for that.
Mom stays in the lodge, reading next to the fire,
while we hit the slopes.

We glide slowly up,
Maya grips the side of the lift,
Neel and Dad swing their ski-tipped feet ahead of us.
I gaze at the mountain,
pristine and bright,
as we move up to the top
of the world.
Up here, there's nothing to worry about,
no performances or tests.
Up here, it's just us
together.
Up here, we're away

from all our worries.
We stand as the lift reaches the top
then glide and turn, glide and turn,
g l i d e and
turn
down and down and down.
like we're floating
like we're flying.

Maya
Down the Mountain

Flying down the hills
in winter sun with Chaya
is sweetest freedom.

Chaya
A New Competition

January, and we're back to school.
Maya shrinks into herself again.
At the end of wind ensemble,
Mr. G asks Maya and me
to stay behind.
The chamber orchestra's having a concert this spring, he says,
and we're planning a special piece for piano and violin.
I'd like you both to audition.

> Maya's face brightens.
> *That's exciting.*

What piece is it? I ask.
A beautiful piece by Arvo Pärt, says Mr. G,
called "Spiegel im Spiegel."
He presses a button on his laptop and we listen.
The song is gorgeous—simple repeated chords,
a lovely dance between piano and strings.
It feels like peace.
This song would be perfect for Maya.
She squeezes my hand, and I know she thinks
it would be perfect for me.

What does
"Spiegel im Spiegel" mean?
she asks.

It's very contemplative, says Mr. G.
It means "Mirror in the Mirror."

Maya's face blanches,
she drops my hand.

You'll have a few weeks to prepare for the audition.
Mr. G hands us sheet music.
There are some older students trying out,
but I think you both have a great shot.
Thanks, Mr. G, I say.

Maya gathers her things
in a hurry,

I rush to keep up.
Jay waits just outside the door.
Auditioning against each other, huh?
Go away, Jay, I say. I turn to Maya.
What's wrong? I say with a look.

The bell rings
she rushes off.

Maya
Mirror in the Mirror

That afternoon when we get home,
Chaya and I watch more videos of
"Spiegel im Spiegel."
The name shocked me,
but the music is
magical.

The piano part is
broken chords
repeated
repeated
repeated
over
and
over,
like a brook
running
like a song
in a dream.

I want Chaya to play it

and I want to play it,

too.

We've always split parts equally,

never competed against each other.

The knowledge

that only one of us can win

stings

like a cut

no one else

can see.

Maya
Fermata

Friday night,
Chaya's in the shower
I go downstairs
for a drink of water,
hear my parents arguing
in whispers.

I do not expect too much! Mom says.

You're too rigid, says Dad.

I want the best for us all, she says.

But you can't require perfection.

I like things in order.

It's too much pressure.
The children feel it, too.

The children are perfectly
fine!
Her words almost a scream.

I turn to run upstairs,
fine echoing
in my head.

Chaya
Silent Storm

I walk into our room fresh from the shower,
cozy in my fluffy robe,
my hair wrapped in a towel.
I hum. My bed is calling me.
But I find Maya curled up,
stiff and gasping,
the air around her thick.
What's wrong? I lay my hand on her arm.

                                    She shakes her head.

What happened? You can tell me.

                                    Her body trembles.

I need to go get Mom and Dad.

                                    No! Please, Chaya.
                                    She starts to cry.

She sobs like the world is ending.
I hold her hand,
my hair drips to mingle with her tears.

Maya
Hurricane

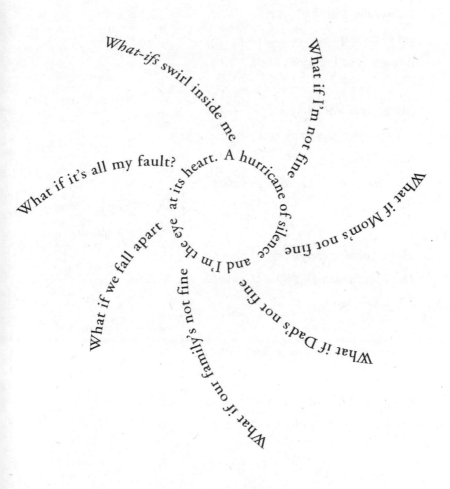

What-ifs swirl inside me

What if I'm not fine

What if it's all my fault?

What if Mom's not fine

at its heart. A hurricane of silence and I'm in the eye

What if Dad's not fine

What if we fall apart

What if our family's not fine

Chaya
Selfish

Maya finally goes silent and still.
I cover her with a blanket,
get dressed quietly,
tiptoe to our bedroom door.

My parents' voices float up
as I go down the stairs and pause
out of sight.
I'm alive, Nalini. I need to feel alive.

> *You're being selfish.*
> *Think of your family.*

You're scared of everything.
Don't shut yourself off from the world,
like your mother.

> *I'm not like my mother!*

I can't keep Maya's secret any longer.
She needs help.
But how can I interrupt them?
I've had enough, Dad says.

What does that mean?
Mom asks.

I'm not arguing anymore tonight.
I'm about to step inside
when two things happen:
Dad stalks from the room
and someone grabs my wrist.

Maya
I Know

In my room my eyes
snap open. And Chaya's gone.
I know where she is
and I can't let her tell them.

Chaya
Betrayed

Maya's face is tight
grip fierce
as she pulls me
back into the hallway
back up the stairs
back to our room
where she closes the door
pins me to the wall with her look.

How could you? she
hisses.

You need help, Maya.

*I don't need help
from Mom or Dad.
They're fighting
all the time!*
She takes a shuddering
breath.

Maya, please, I say.

*You've shown me I can't
trust you.
Now leave me alone.*

Her voice is cold,
frozen.
She turns her back
gets in bed
switches off the light.

Her secret's eating her up
and all I can do is watch.

Maya
I'll Do It

I can't let Chaya tell Mom and Dad
about my secret.
If I'm not fine,
it will drive them more apart.
And then the broken mirror
will have won.

I just need to hold on until August,
when the seven years' bad luck
will finally be over.
Then this worry
will be over, too.

But now Chaya's shown me
I need to keep my secret
from her, too.
I can't show her
I'm hurting.
It won't be easy,
but I'll do it.

Chaya
Let's Play

When Dad comes home the next evening,
Mom won't talk to him.
After dinner, Neel says,
Let's play Sorry.

Maya
Sorry

Neel draws a card.
Sorry, he says,
sending Dad back to Start.
Dad draws a card.
Sorry, he tells Mom.
But you didn't draw a Sorry card, says Neel.
Mom draws a card. *Sorry*, she tells Dad.
You don't know how to play this game, says Neel.
Chaya draws a card and looks at me.
Sorry, she says.
But I don't say it back.

Chaya
Forced Silence

The next day, and the next day and the next,
Maya won't talk to me.
A week later, and not a word between us.
Maya chats with Neel in the car,
sits with Jay and Abby on the bus.
At our piano lesson, Mrs. Yu plays Debussy.
The music sounds like an Impressionist painting,
but also sounds too hard to me.
Maya says we'll play it
without even looking my way.
Neel asks us to build with Legos,
and if I say yes, Maya won't join in.
At night, she listens to music
with her earbuds in.
There's no singing, no before-bed
games of What If.

But our parents are too absorbed
in their own silence
to pay attention to ours.

Maya
For Her Sake

Before the audition
for "Spiegel im Spiegel"
I go to the bathroom,
press C C C C C C C into my palm
where Chaya can't see.
I can't let her know anymore,
for her sake.
For all our sakes.
The bad luck must stop with me.

Chaya
Phantom Limb

People say when someone loses an arm, a leg
sometimes they can still feel it,
a gnawing echo of former flesh and bone.
That's what it's like,
the phantom limb
where my twin
used to be.

Alone in our room, I wonder
why did she fall apart that night?
I look at my latest math test, where I got a perfect score.
I sneak into Maya's folder, pull hers out:
98.

I think about the marks on her hand: C C C C C C C
. . . for *Chaya*?

Is it not about her grade,	but my grade?
not about her piano playing,	but my playing?
not about trying to be perfect,	but more perfect than me?
Does my existence	make her worse?
Have I been the shadow	hurting her all along?

I put my head in my hands.

I've always loved
sharing everything with Maya.
But maybe I'm the phantom limb   making her ache.

So I decide to change
the only thing I can:
Me.

Sometimes you have to leap.

Part Two
SWITCH

Chaya
Not Quite Identical

I tuck my hair into my knit cap before breakfast
and Neel notices.
How come I have to take off my baseball cap,
but you get to wear that in the house? he asks.
I'm cold, I say.   Though not as cold as Maya's been.
Not fair, says Neel.
Life's not fair, I say and snatch a piece of toast.
I love him, but he's like a little dog
that won't give up a ball.
Mom! How come Chaya gets to—
Drop it. I shoot him a glare.

                                  What is it, Neel? We need to leave
                                  in five minutes,
                                  Mom says, frantically packing
                                  Neel's lunch.

I scoot to Neel and whisper:
Just drop it and I'll take you to the park
tomorrow after school.
Why not today? he whines.
We have piano. But we can go tomorrow.
For a long time, I promise.

His mouth curves up, his dark eyes sparkle.

I can climb to the top of the monkey bars!

I nod. It will be freezing,

but I know how to bribe him.

Maya gives me a look.

I ignore her.

Time to go, Mom says.

We grab jackets, slip on boots

pile into the car.

At our lockers Maya glances at my cap,

but I dash away

before she asks a question.

In homeroom, I pull it off,

let my hair spill over my shoulders.

My wavy, black hair. Just like Maya's.

Except now it has a thick pink streak

going down the right side.

Kids look up. Anisa beams a smile.

Now no one can say they can't tell us apart.

And this is just the start.

Maya
Hide-and-Seek

I hide,
and you find me.
I seek,
and I find you.
You've always been there,
since before we had memories
and we floated in the watery dark together,
with no need to breathe.
We knew each other
before anyone else knew us,
before we knew we existed
as ourselves.
I shut you out.
I'm sorry.
And now I'll find my way
back.

Chaya
What Did You Do?

Maya asks as she slides her tray
between Anisa's and mine.

After a week of silence,
I've made her find her voice.
I need a change of pace.
I bite my chicken sandwich—extra zesty,
just like my new hair.
Charming, says Anisa. *I love it.* She nibbles a fry.
But how'd your parents let you do it?
Thanks, Anstounding One, I say.
And . . . they don't exactly know.
Anisa giggles nervously. *Oh man, are you going to get in trouble?*
It's my hair, I say with false confidence.
I can do what I want with it.

Mom is going to kill you.
Maya touches her hair as if making sure
it hasn't changed, too.
But why—

Why what?

Why didn't you tell me?
Because you haven't been talking to me!

I want to scream.

Because you would have tried to stop me. Right?

Maya shrugs.

I finish my sandwich, enjoying every bite.

Maya hasn't

touched hers.

Maya
Advice

It's clear that Chaya's taken to heart
Dad's advice to be bold.

Chaya
The Next Step

I find Mr. G in the music room before my next class.

Great to see you . . . Chaya? he says.

  I nod.

The "Spiegel im Spiegel" decision will be posted Wednesday.

How can I help you?

  I swallow.

  I'm withdrawing my name from the audition, I say.

May I ask why?

  I take a breath.

  Just . . . not interested anymore.

All right, if that's what you want. He frowns.

Are you okay, Chaya? Anything I can help with?

  I'm fine. I glance at the dear cluttered room.

  And I'm quitting wind ensemble.

Maya
Disharmony

Chaya and I would sing our tune
of school and friends,
of cocoa in the morning
and tea in the afternoon,
of math and English and science class,
of school days and summer camp,
of books and movies, TV shows,
of music everywhere.
Our voices identical, blended,
perfectly in sync.
But what happens
when your partner
starts to sing a different song?
What happens to the duet
when one of us stops singing?

Chaya
A New Song

In pickup line after school, Jay's eyes are drawn
to the pink streak in my hair.
He takes a step back.
Like it? I shake my head so it swishes.
Sure, he says. *Why not?*

                    Now Maya shakes her head,
                    makes her ponytail bounce.

A silver SUV pulls up
the window opens and Vimala Auntie's voice blares:
Jay, raja, get in the car. We need to get to your science—
Oh! Maya-Chaya, hello, she says.
Her smile's red but fake, her earrings real but gaudy.
Hello, Auntie, we say in unison.
Auntie looks at me and does a double take.
Maya?

                    That's me. Maya raises her hand.
Chaya, then. What have you—
Let's get going, Mom. Jay opens the door, climbs in.
We don't want to be late.
I can see the gossip gears start turning in Auntie's head
as she presses her lips in a thin line.

Mom pulls up in our green minivan.
Maya and I climb in, and Neel yells,
Chaya! Why's your hair a funny color?

>Mom turns to us. Her eyes widen
>in surprise.
>*Chee! Why would you put that awful*
>*color in your hair?*
>*We don't have time before piano,*
>*but you must wash it out as soon as we*
>*get home!*

Neel puts his hands over his ears.   Maya winces.
It'll wear off in a few weeks, I say.
It's only semi-permanent.

>*A few weeks? Semi-permanent?*
>Mom glares at me in the rearview
>mirror
>*Your birthday is coming. We'll be going to*
>*the temple.*
>*Chaya, what were you thinking?*

I just wanted a change of pace.
It sounds silly now.

>*If you can't wash it out,*
>*we'll dye your hair*
>*back to its normal color.*
>*See?* Maya says with her look.

I stare out my window, chew my lip
in the silence that follows.
What I know:
I'm not changing my hair back.
What I don't know:
how to face Mrs. Yu's disappointment
when I tell her I'm quitting.

Maya
Wrong Notes

Mrs. Yu nods
as I play the first part of "Clair de Lune."
I stumble, start again
stumble, start again
and yet again.
Take it more slowly, Maya.
You don't want to keep practicing the wrong notes
or they will get stuck in your fingers.
I listen and do better.
When we're finished, we go out to the lobby of the music studio,
where Neel is glued to a tablet
and Mom and Chaya are waiting, arms crossed,
not looking at each other.
Chaya, come in, says Mrs. Yu, barely glancing at Chaya's hair.
Mrs. Yu grows annoyed if we let our nails grow too long
and they click against the keys.
She'll make Chaya return to herself.
She won't let her keep playing the wrong notes,
won't let them get stuck.

Chaya
A Piacere

I brace myself
for anger, guilt.

My parents have already paid
for my lessons this semester,
and quitting now means a waste
of money,
of talent,
of the time I've spent.

Before I lose my nerve, I say, *I want to quit piano.*

I almost take it back.
But then I remember Maya curled up
in the storm of her panic,
and I know I must quit.
For her.
                    But Mrs. Yu hasn't responded.
I risk a glance out of the corner of my eye.
                    You were saying? she says.
I want to quit, I repeat.

Mrs. Yu nods. *Yes, Chaya. But why?*
Is Debussy not to your liking?

I'm sick of music, I lie.

Mrs. Yu smiles.
I don't believe that for a minute. What's
really going on?
I'm not going to pressure you. I just want
to understand.

I wasn't prepared for this.
I can't tell her about Maya
without betraying her confidence.
But I owe Mrs. Yu an explanation,
to quit suddenly
after years learning music from her.
So I reach for the lame phrase I said about my hair:
I need a change of pace.
I slump on the bench, stare at the gleaming keys
I still love so much.

I understand, says Mrs. Yu.
I gape at her. *You . . . do?*

Yes, she says.
But that doesn't mean you have to quit
piano.

But—

Are you familiar with the term
"a piacere"?

I blink. *No . . .*

>*It's an instruction.*
>*To play at your own pleasure.*

I don't understand.

>*Consider it . . . a metaphor.*
>*What about changing the type of music*
>*you play?*

What?

>*You could play contemporary music,*
>*or try composition.*

None of this has occurred to me.
We spend the rest of the lesson
picking through more modern music,
and a book on beginning composition.
And just like that, Mrs. Yu
has saved me from myself.
Maybe I don't need to give up music completely.
As I stand to leave, she says softly,

>*I also have a sister.*

Maya
Abandoned

When Chaya emerges with Mrs. Yu,
her eyes are bright, her shoulders relaxed,
a smile plays upon her face.
Nalini, Mrs. Yu says, *I gave Chaya some new music today.*

> *Oh*, says Mom.

*She's interested in playing more contemporary music
and trying composition, so we've started on that.*

> *They're playing different
> kinds of music now?*
> Mom asks.

*Yes, Chaya feels strongly about it,
and I want my students to play
what they're passionate about.*
Mom nods and stands,
Chaya pats her pink streak,
and I see I've been abandoned.
Chaya's getting what she wants,
and for the first time ever,
we don't want the same thing.

Chaya
Simmer to Boiling

It's teatime
and I'm in hot water.

> *She must make her hair normal,* Mom says
> as she dips a Gluco biscuit in her mug.

Dad takes a handful of spicy mixture and crunches.

She's almost thirteen. This is normal.
And harmless. Right, kanna? He looks at me.

> *It's disrespectful,* Mom says.

How is it disrespectful? I manage to ask.

> Mom sips her tea, frowns.
> *It's not natural,* she says.

Your hair isn't completely natural anymore,
is it? Dad asks with a wink.
I know mine isn't.

> Mom stiffens.
> *That's not the same.*

It's exactly the same. You and I
show the world what we want to.
Just like when I give my patients
a beautiful set of new, straight teeth.

Chaya is doing the same.
Thanks, Dad, I murmur.

          But you and Mom are adults, Maya says.

          That's correct. Children are supposed
          to listen to their elders, Mom says.

The elders don't agree
on what I should do, I say.

          Chaya, don't be obstinate, says Mom.

She's not the one being obstinate,
Dad replies.

          You don't believe in rules.

          Mom puts her cup down.

          You think everything is jokes and games
          and adventures.

Jokes and games and adventures
took us pretty far.
Where's the girl
who used to love to ride behind me
on my motorcycle? Where's she hiding?

Mom used to ride on a motorcycle?
I force myself to close my mouth.

Dad leans to take Mom's hand,
but she pulls away.

We're not children
anymore, Shreedhar.
We have a family. We
can't always be joking
and fooling around.
Dad puts down his cup. *Nalini, don't start.*
My stomach churns.
Please don't argue. Not because of me, I think.

You're the one
who always starts, says Mom,
I'm the one
who creates order from your chaos.
Order out of chaos, huh? Dad says sharply.
Maya and I lock eyes.
We grab Neel,
bundle up, head out the back door
while Mom and Dad's argument
goes from a simmer
to a rapid boil.

Maya
From Up High

We step outside
into the waning light
of the winter day,
our maple's branches stark and bare.
We start to climb, and Neel goes so fast
it's more like he's leaping from branch to branch.
Chaya and I follow more slowly
until we're all up high.
I hate it when they argue, Chaya says.

> *Daddy's right*, says Neel.
>
> *I like your hair.*
>
>> *But would it be so bad*
>> *if you changed back?* I ask.

Chaya pauses, watching the cold sun
preparing to drop.
I'd like to keep it.
My hair, and the new things I'm trying.

> *Yay!* Neel claps his hands.
>
>> *Neel, don't let go of the branch!*
>> I warn.
>
> Neel grabs hold again and pouts.

Okay, I say to Chaya. *If that's what you want.*

Thanks, Chaya says.

She's looking at me steadily, the other half of me,
sitting just across the tree,
surrounded by bare branches, dim light
like a halo.

If this makes her happy,
I can live with it,
I think.

Why do you like climbing so much, Neel? Chaya asks.

I like the climbing part, but
I also like looking at the world
from up high, he says.

Me too, Chaya says.   *Me three*, I say.

We linger in the twilight,
the three of us together.
Looking at the world from up high.

Chaya
The Same Side

We only climb down when the sun has sunk so low
the sky is inky blue.

Remember the rules, Maya says
to Neel.

Yes, Maya Akka. Not too high,
and not in the dark or rain, he says dully.

And never alone, Maya says.
Someone needs to know
where you are.

Why do you always boss me?
I can't wait to be big,
then I can climb whatever I want
and no one can stop me, Neel says
as we drop to the frozen ground.

I put my arm
around his skinny shoulders.
Even when you're big,
we'll still be your big sisters.

Maya puts her arm around him
from the other side.

Always.

Our arms touch. I hope we can stay
on the same side.

Maya
Success

I win the audition.
I'll play the piano part in "Spiegel im Spiegel"
with Albert, an eighth-grade violinist,
the best in the school.
Mr. G congratulates me,
students murmur *good job*,
Anisa smiles,
Jay gives me a piercing look
from across the room.
My heart lifts for a moment
but then we're back to work,
rehearsing.
I have wind ensemble music,
my piece for Mrs. Yu,
and "Spiegel im Spiegel"
to perfect
for the spring.
I try to recapture that heart-lifting moment
but cracks creep into the corners
of my world.
I won,

but it's more work.
I won,
but Chaya's not here
to share it.
I'm not sure this feels
like success.

Chaya
She's Fine

Maya's late for lunch.

I spot Jay at our table and almost don't sit down.

What's up with Maya? Jay asks.

I'm sure she'll be here soon, I say. Where's Anisa when I need her?

I don't mean today, says Jay.

I mean . . . in general.

My eyes narrow. He gets his nosiness from his mom.

I don't know what you're talking about.

Come on, Chaya.

She's always been a little anxious,

but lately . . .

I don't know what you're talking about, I lie again.

If Jay knows,

he might tell Vimala Auntie.

Then everyone

will know.

Let me know if I can help,

he says.

He's always trying to get between me and my twin.

She's fine, I say as Maya and Anisa show up.

If I say it out loud, I can make it true.

Maya
Lost

We're ten,
playing hide-and-seek with Jay
and a handful of neighborhood kids.
Jay is It,
and as he counts,
we scatter
and I lose Chaya in the scramble.
I crouch behind a neighbor's thorny hedge,
certain that no seeker will risk scratches
to find me there.
Someone is captured
and we all come in.
All except Chaya.
Clouds gather overhead,
we trickle home in twos and threes.
Jay tugs at me
but where is Chaya?
We look for her,
call her name,
but she doesn't answer.
It's going to rain, Jay says.

She's gone home. Let's go.
There's a growing churning in my stomach,
staccato tapping in my chest,
as we hurry home.
Lightning flashes,
rain pours,
and Chaya's not at home.
A sharp pain cracks my wrist.
I clutch it and cry
for Chaya,
lost and hurt.

Chaya
Mano Sinistra

We're ten, playing hide-and-seek,
and I climb a tree
to avoid being caught by Jay.
I nestle into the crook between two big branches
I wait and wait and   wait
and somehow fall asleep.
I open my eyes to voices.
She's gone home. Let's go, says Jay.

                     I don't know, says Maya.

I'm about to surprise them from above, when—
There's no way she's still out here.
We've been looking all this time.
She ditched us, says Jay.
I'm so mad I can't speak.

                 Chaya and I don't ditch each
                 other.

That's right, Maya!
Come on. It's about to rain. You know she's at your house, says Jay.
I wait for Maya to say no.
But after a while, I realize
they've gone.

Because of Jay.

Lightning cracks, thunder booms,
my anger gives way to fear.
It reminds me of the stormy night when Neel was born
and almost died.
I'm lightning-lit,
thunder-shaken,
as rain starts to fall in sheets.
I scramble down, lose my grip
on a slippery limb,
   fall
      hear a crack

   run home
to find Maya crying,
clutching her left arm.
The one that I've broken.

Maya
Pause

Chaya's wrist is swollen and tender.
We go to the hospital
where I'm so worried
and she's so brave
through poking,
through prodding,
through x-rays.

Jay comes with us,
lends me quiet strength
while Neel asks nonstop questions
and Dad teases
that he expected Neel to be the first
to crack a limb.

Mom stops squeezing my hand so tightly
once the cast is on
and Chaya closes her eyes
to rest.
But I'm full of dread.

I shouldn't have left Chaya alone.
I think of all the *what-ifs*:
broken writing hand,
broken leg,
broken neck.
I let my guard down,
and Chaya suffered.
She broke her wrist,
but I'm the one who's broken.

Dad's phone rings—
Vimala Auntie.
And in the pause,
held just a bit too long,
I know
nothing will ever
be the same.

Dad listens
and his face blanches.
He takes Jay's hand,
makes him sit,
hands the phone to him.
Keerthi Uncle's heart gave out
and I know it's my fault

the bad luck moved
to someone else I love.
To Jay.

Chaya
Auditions

I shift on my feet waiting to audition
for the spring musical, *Fiddler on the Roof.*
Without wind ensemble,
I need to find a way
to make music with others.
I don't care what part,
I just want to be part   of something.
I've memorized a speech,
practiced "Sunrise, Sunset"
until I sing it in my sleep.
I've never tried out for a big production
because Maya never wanted to.
Now I'm alone
in the midst of theater kids
who all know each other.

Fiddler's about love,
music, conflict
between parents and children.
And five sisters!
One sister's all I ever wanted,

and I've grown apart from her.

Ms. Dalton calls my name,
I say my speech, and then
it's time to sing—
a few of us together,
and then some solo lines.
I think I'm doing okay—
I like this kind of music.
But I'm so used to hearing
Maya's touch on the keys,
her voice in my head,
that a pang shoots through my chest,
my voice wavers,
and I blow it.

My footsteps echo on the wooden floor
as I make my way offstage.

Maya
Stage Fright

I can't imagine anything worse
than auditioning for a play
except
auditioning for a musical.
I can't understand
slipping into a character's skin
using my own voice.
Ever since first grade,
when we sang and acted
"Señor Don Gato" and Chaya volunteered me
to be the Fluffy White Cat
and I froze right in the middle
of my "Meow-Meow-Meow,"
I've avoided being onstage.
It's not at all
like playing piano,
where it's the instrument
that speaks,
that sings.

Maya
Ditched

At wind ensemble,
Anisa's eyes keep moving to me
and I know she's missing Chaya.
I miss her, too.
I miss her whispers in my ear
about who's playing well,
who's acting up,
who's Most Clueless in the room.
I even miss her snide asides
about Jay.
I started this,
but I never thought
she'd stay away.

Chaya
No Going Back

The callback list is posted the next day.
I search the names
and mine isn't on it.
My bubble of hope
pops.
I'll be in the chorus,
singing ensemble pieces,
with barely a line of dialogue.
I tell myself it's not surprising—
the kids cast in big roles
have all been doing theater forever,
while I'm just starting.

I've given up wind ensemble,
classical piano,
for this.
I want to go back to playing Mozart, Bach, Holst,
Debussy.
I want to practice "Spiegel im Spiegel"
again.
I want to play music

with Anisa, with Maya.

But without me, Maya will get to shine.
In wind ensemble, with Mrs. Yu,
playing with the best violinist in the school.
I'll stay in the shadows   if she enjoys the spotlight.

There's no going back.

Maya
My Fault

Chaya's quit everything
we used to do together
and I know
it's all my fault.
I pushed her away,
put new silence between us.
But
she's happy
trying new things
I don't want to try.

At night I ask, *What if
we went back to how things used
to be?*

She doesn't answer

and I realize
I never said the words out loud.

Chaya
Love and Like

Dad and I make cocoa together
on a Saturday afternoon.
A pink mug for you, says Dad,
to match your hair.
I laugh and add extra marshmallows.
Mom likes the mug, but not my hair, I say.
Or me.
She loves you, says Dad.
But she doesn't like me right now, I say.
There's a difference.

He pauses, exhales.
Your mom likes knowing what to expect.
Change can be hard, but it's important—
otherwise, we can get stuck.
Just give her time,
and she'll get used to it.

Maya
Whispers

At the temple, after singing songs of praise
and asking God for blessings
Neel goes off to play,
Dad joins the men,
and Mom, Chaya, and I
drift through the clumps of women,
talking talking talking
about whose sari is prettiest
whose child got into college
who did something shocking.
What was she thinking
How can they allow it
Such disrespect.

Chaya doesn't care,
but all I know
is I never want to be the subject
of these whispers.

Chaya
Begin Again

It's not easy to begin again
halfway through seventh grade.
I'm jealous of the wind ensemble musicians
playing Brahms and Sibelius,
but at least I'm seeing less
of Jay.
I'm making new friends, theater kids:
Bailey—dark-haired, dimpled, Tzeitel in the play;
Parker—fellow chorus member;
and Jordan—on tech crew, doing lighting.

The silence between me and Maya
is easy,
easier than I ever thought it would be.
We barely see each other in class
or on the bus.
Half the time, she gets off at Jay's house
instead of coming home.
I wanted distance, but
maybe not this much.
But Maya's storms of panic

are less frequent, I think.
So I see more of Anisa,
hang out with Neel,
a solitary twin.

Maya
What's Really Going On

I can't concentrate on studying.

I miss Chaya, I say.

I'm not sure
I feel the same way? says Jay.

A giggle bursts from my mouth
against my will.
But then I press into my palm:
C C C C C C
Can't believe she's abandoned me.

She's just trying something new.

C C C C C C

Stop scratching, he says.
Don't hurt yourself.
He takes my hand
sees the marks I've made
his warm brown eyes
are wide.
What's really going on?

My hand stings as I pull away.
Let's go back to social studies.

Chaya
Sharing

Maya and I no longer need to share
the piano parts in wind ensemble,
but we still need to share
the piano.
I pull out the sheet music from *Fiddler*,
play from the first song, "Tradition."
I won't be playing it onstage,
but I want to analyze it,
see how it's put together.

> Maya comes in, stops short.
> *How long are you going to be?*

Just got here.
At least forty-five minutes, I say.

> She huffs.
> *I've got music for Mrs. Yu,*
> *wind ensemble,*
> *chamber orchestra.*
> *And a ton of homework tonight.*

I got here first.

> *Fine.*
> She crosses her arms,

stalks from the room.

The next day after school
I find a signup sheet for the piano.
It's so *Maya* that I laugh.
But I take a pen and claim my time.

Maya
Fine

Mom, I say one night
as she tidies the kitchen
Can I help?
I mean much more
than cleaning up.

She takes so long to answer
I wonder if she's heard.
I'm fine, kanna, she says.
Everything is fine.
Just keep being your perfect self.
She scrubs the counter
rubs at a stain that no one else
can see.

Chaya
Scary

Dad's going away for three days
ice fishing with a friend.
Can I come? Neel asks.
Sorry, son. Grown-ups only. It's too cold for you.

               Too cold for you, too, says Mom.
               Must you go?
               Maya hovers, watching.

Dad pats his belly.
Plenty of padding here. Not like you,
little chicken!
Dad tickles, Neel screeches.

               Mom sighs. *Be careful.*
               Come back safe.

I'm always careful.

               Maya stays still and silent.
Dad's just going fishing with a friend.
Why is this so scary?

               Maya tries to hide it, but I know
               she's scratching her hand again.
It's only a matter of time   before it bleeds.

Maya
Idea

Abby catches me in the hall.
Are you going on any tours? she asks.

> *Tours of what?*

Boarding schools, of course.
She tosses her chestnut hair, gives me a sideways glance.
We start applying in the fall,
so it's better to narrow down
where you want to go ahead of time.

> *Boarding schools?*
> I say dumbly.

Abby leans forward and whispers.
My mom and her whole family
have always gone to Evergreen,
so I have a great shot at getting in there.
But I want to look at others.
I don't know why she's telling me.
She's always made me feel
like I'm the competition.

> *What do you think?*
> I ask Jay.
> *About boarding school?*

He shrugs. *You know my brother went to Walden.*
It might be nice to go away.

I think of the times when Chaya and I
are happiest.
It's when we're away—
on vacation,
at Camp Allegro.
I walk to class,
ideas flooding me
like waves of music.

Chaya
Hypothetically

I'm over at Anisa's, listening to music
as we do homework.

> *I miss you in wind ensemble*, she says.

I miss you, too. How's Maya?

> *Wouldn't you know better than me?* she
> asks.

We're not . . . talking that much lately.

> Anisa nods.

> *You don't have to tell me, but does Maya . . .*
> *worry? A lot?*
> *Hypothetically, of course.*

Hypothetically . . . maybe?

> *Well, hypothetically,*
> *I can tell you I know what it feels*
> *like.*
> *It's been hard for me*
> *for years.*

I nod.

> *But some things have made it*
> *better.*

Anisa talks,
I listen.
Hypothetically, of course.

Maya
Help

Chaya's spending the night at Anisa's,
and Dad,
back safely from his fishing trip,
reads in the living room
while I practice piano after dinner.
I'm playing Mozart,
not Debussy—
which I don't want to play without Chaya.
Beautiful, he says.

> *I made a dozen mistakes.*
> I sit on my hands.

Mistakes are just the beginning
of getting things right, he says.

> I shake my head.
> *I can't afford mistakes.*

At least this kind isn't expensive, he says.
Not like that time I scraped the car
backing out of the garage.

> A laugh and a gasp fight each other
> in my throat.

Maya kanna, is there something
bothering you?
Can I help?
Dad's voice is gentle, serious
for once.

> I swallow.
> Dad has no fear
> so how can I tell him about mine?
> I shake my head,
> play the piece again.
> Only eleven mistakes this time.

Chaya
Breathe

When Maya bangs the piano keys again
I sit with her on the bench.
I learned something in play rehearsal, I say,
that helps us with our singing posture.
It might help you, too.

> Maya shrugs her shoulders,
> sits on her hands.
> *Okay,* she says. *I'll try it.*

I show her:
Feet on ground,
hands on knees,
spine straight,
eyes closed.
Breathe, I say.
One-two-three-four-five-six-seven in,
one-two-three-four-five-six-seven out.
We breathe together
in sync once again.
She doesn't need to know
I learned to breathe this way from Anisa.

Maya
Hide

The storms of silence
still descend
still fill my ears
with a roar
no one else can hear.
What if
What if
What if
What if
What if
What if
What if
What
If

I'm just better
at hiding them.

Chaya
Twin Telepathy

The alarm goes off
and before I even open my eyes
I say, *Happy Birthday, Maya.*

                        Happy Birthday, Chaya, she replies.

I grab the small package
go to Maya's bed   where she's already sitting up.
Our gifts look almost
the same size.
Exactly, in fact.
I tear my package.   Maya unwraps hers carefully.
No way, I breathe, and hold up
a thin silver chain with a pendant—
a curvy letter *C* nestling a brilliant purple gem,
an amethyst, our February birthstone.

                        Maya opens her box, gasps, giggles.
                        Did you ask Mom?

Never. I laugh, fall over
on the bed.
I've gotten Maya the same pendant
with a curvy *M.*
I used all my holiday money,

did extra chores to pay for it.
When I saw it in the gift shop in Vermont
I knew I had to get it.

                        And clearly, so did she.

I scoot over, hug her tight.

                        My sister.

We've often felt connected   by twin telepathy.
But this year it feels extra special—
this year,
when we've grown   apart.

Maya
Thirteen

Thirteen,
we start the day together,
our first words just for each other.
I laugh at our twin telepathy
that made us choose the same gifts.
Doesn't she see
that we are the same?
Doesn't she see
that she shouldn't change?

Thirteen, and it's almost like
the past few weeks haven't happened,
like we're playing the same music again.
Thirteen, and the seven years' bad luck
is almost over.
We just have to finish the summer,
and we're free.

Chaya
Third Wheel

In homeroom I hand out Mom's cupcakes and laddoos,
> *Can't wait for tonight, Charmpion,*
> says Anisa, biting into red velvet.
Warning, Anstouding: Jay's coming, too, I say.
> *Chool,* says my easygoing friend.
He doesn't bug you?
> *He's fine. Why does he bother you so*
> *much?*
I chew my lip, think for a moment.
It's his birthday, too. For years, we've celebrated together.
Maybe I'm sick of having a third wheel.
Besides, his mom can't stop talking about how perfect he is.
The scientist! The trumpet maestro!
And I can't stand how he parts his hair.
> Anisa giggles.

I sigh.

Maya
Dental Humor

That night at our favorite Chinese restaurant,
Dad opens fortune cookies
and tells terrible jokes
to Neel and his friend Sam.
You will take a long trip . . .
to the other side of the universe,
in a boat made of cornflakes, he says to Sam.
As long as you don't land in the Milky Way,
you'll be all right.
Sam and Neel giggle, Anisa snickers, Jay snorts,
Chaya groans, I roll my eyes.
And you . . . he says to Neel,
will come upon a mountain of gummy worms,
but you must fight fears of tooth decay,
and eat your way through them.
Dad winks.
And then, you'll need to use
the world's longest roll of dental floss,
and that is how you make it
into the world record books!
Neel grins, showing off

his two missing teeth.
I'm going to climb the highest mountains,
made of candy and floss and candy floss,
and that's how I'll set the world record!
Of course our little brother invents
new kinds of things to climb.

                    Mom smiles,
                    her worry lines smoothed out.

But Vimala Auntie gives Dad
such a look of sadness
it makes my chest ache.

Chaya
Thirteen Candles

Mom's made our favorite carrot cake,
light and fluffy
with tiny bits of pineapple
heavenly cream cheese frosting
and a hint of lemon zest.

It would be better without walnuts,
says Vimala Auntie.
We nutty twins love walnuts, I say.
Her face twists,
and I smile sweetly.
We take photos,
and then we need to take more
with Jay and *his* cake—
a luscious chocolate-raspberry creation
from our favorite local bakery.
How can Vimala Auntie criticize Mom's cake
when she didn't even bake her own?
I give Maya a look   but she won't return it.
Anisa shrugs.

Thirteen candles blaze.

I close my eyes,
hope my plan has worked,
that shaking things up
has helped Maya enough.
Thirteen candles
light up Maya's face.
We blow them out
and shadows return.
Thirteen candles.
For the first time in my life,
I wonder what my twin wishes.

Maya
Wish

I close my eyes and make a wish,
for things to return
to how they used to be,
to have my sister back with me.

The next day
when our friends are gone,
we open presents from our parents:
clothes and nail polish and
sparkling earrings,
a painting of our family from Neel,
with twin stick figures dressed alike.
And then
a keyboard with two pairs of headphones
for us both.
But I know who it's really for—
Chaya.
So we no longer have to take turns,
so she can play the keyboard in our room,
practice without competing.

My heart flutters like a trill that's way too slow
at the delight in Chaya's eyes.

And I know for sure
my wish will not come true.

Maya
Haunted

The Chamber Orchestra concert is next week—
and my duet with Albert
on "Mirror in the Mirror."
I'm haunted by that mirror
from long ago.
I must be perfect
or what other bad thing will happen?
I press my nail into my palm:
C C C C C C C
but only when
Chaya isn't
looking.

Chaya
Mirror in the Mirror

If I had a magic mirror,
I'd reflect to Maya
the packed auditorium,
the hushed thrill of the crowd,
Mom and Dad dressed up, holding hands,
Neel in a blue bow tie,
my fingers tingling
with the memory of notes I practiced
but won't play.
I'd reflect to her my wish
that she plays like I know she can.
I'd show her what she looks like,
the other half of me,
wearing blue velvet,
hair up, so elegant.
I'd reflect her and Albert,
eyes locked,
fingers ready,
bow poised.
I'd reflect her caress of the keys,
lilting broken chords,
bass and treble,

violin rising, falling,
yearning, plaintive,
the echoes of their music, reassuring
that all will be okay.
I'd reflect the faces of the crowd, transported
to a place of calm and beauty.
I'd reflect my tears,
inspired by flawless playing.

As the piece comes to a close,
I'd reflect the silent audience
afraid to pop the spell cast over us.
Then the roar of the applause,
the standing ovation,
the wave of love radiating
to them,
to her.
My certainty
that I was right to step away,
that she was born to play
this piece,
the fierce joy in her eyes
as she takes her bow.

If I had a magic mirror,
that's what I'd reflect.

Maya
Bask

Mom and Dad beam
Chaya hands me flowers
Neel hugs me around my waist.
Perfection, kanna, Mom whispers.
I bask in their love for a moment
although I know
it wasn't perfect.

I itch
to press my nail
into my hand
but Chaya takes it.

Chaya
Wild

We have the money, Dad says.

> *It's not about money,* Mom says.
> *It's about safety.*

I know how to ride a motorcycle.
I grew up riding one in India, remember?

> *It's faster, more dangerous here.*
> *After what happened to Keerthi*
> *I'm shocked you'd take this risk.*

Keerthi died of a heart attack,
not a motorcycle accident, Dad says.

> *Two years later,*
> *Vimala and her sons still mourn.*
> *Your family needs you.*
> *Why would you jeopardize*
> *your life for a joy ride?*

I need to feel alive, Dad says.

> *Don't be reckless, like*
> *your daughter,*
> *abandoning her music.*

She's young. She wants to explore.

Vimala says Chaya's too wild,
threatening her future,
and we should make her behave
before she goes too far.
We won't crush our daughter's spirit
based on gossip.

I draw back, shut out their voices.
I'm not the one
they should worry about.

Maya
Onstage

With March comes
opening night of the musical.
The crowd murmurs,
Neel jiggles,
his knee bumping my thigh
like an eager puppy.
Mom's and Dad's faces are alight
with anticipation.

The overture's an appetizer
of all the tunes to come.
The story:
two parents
five daughters
trying to hold on to tradition
in a world that's set against them.
Chaya has a small line as a shopkeeper
and she's part of the chorus—
although she blends well
with the others,
I hear her voice.

Onstage
she is radiant,
inhabiting her role
like that long dress, apron,
headscarf,
are hers,
not a costume.

Onstage
my sister looks at home.
*Matchmaker, matchmaker
make me a match.*
It's clear that she's found hers.

Onstage
she glows.
I ignore the pang
of missing her.
Chaya steps into the light
and shines.

Chaya
Different

A play is different every night.
It's never perfect,
but mishaps and mistakes are part of the fun.
A flubbed line from Tevye saved by Bailey as Tzeitel,
a lost prop,
a spotlight on the wrong actor—
they only add to the energy
of performing live.
At last, we strike the set,
relief mingled with regret
that it's over.
But I look around at new friends:
Jordan, Bailey, Parker, Jack.
Friends I never would have made,
never would've made time for
if I hadn't tried to leap.
We strike the set
to make way
for the next performance.
A play is different every night,
and I am different, too.

Maya
Apart

Spring tiptoes in with April
and we get a week off school.
The maple tree has seeds again,
twin clusters
preparing to fly.
Neel's careful not to hurt them
as he climbs.
Dad's stopped his talk of motorcycles
but wants to try bungee jumping.
Mom argues with him
late into the night.
I don't share my worries
with Chaya.
She re-dyes her pink streak,
spends hours with her new friends.
We live in the same house,
but she lives
as far from me as possible.
Even when we're together,
we're apart.

Chaya
Camp Plans

We can't wait
for our fifth year at Camp Allegro.
Set in the woods of Maine,
it nurtures
all kinds of music.
We loved it from the moment
we saw the cabins by the lake,
met fellow musicians
like birds from different places
who found they spoke
the same language.

Camp forms arrive.
Maya and I have always signed up for the same things:
piano lessons, small chamber groups, wind ensemble.
But I think of Maya taking her bow after
"Spiegel im Spiegel,"
the looseness in her shoulders,
the pride in her eyes.
I want to see her like that
all summer

without her shadow.
So I look at other options:
voice lessons, composition,
musical theater.

Maya asks to see my forms.
Will she admit that things are better,
now that I'm no longer her shadow?
                              Maybe I'll try jazz, she says.
My face burns. *With Jay?*
                              Hope so. She sets her jaw.
Good for you, I say,
not thinking it's good at all.
                              Maya fills out her forms in silence
                              silence that lasts all day.

Maya
In the Morning

We open our eyes just the same in the morning.
These weeks feel like such a strange game in the morning.

My sister, she sings like a lark in the morning.
The look that she gives me, so dark in the morning.

She tosses her bedsheets aside in the morning.
She puts on her armor to hide in the morning.

I miss her identical smile in the morning.
But I'm stuck on my separate isle in the morning.

I feel so apart from my twin in the morning.
Can't think of how to begin in the morning.

We used to be fully in sync, day and night.
And now she believes that I'm wrong, and she's right.

We open our eyes just the same.
                    It's like mourning.

Maya
Alone

On a weekend walk with Jay

How're you doing? he asks.

I inhale slowly
one-two-three-four-five-six-seven
and the air is warm, almost.
I tell him I'm playing Mozart
for our spring recital with Mrs. Yu.
Chaya's playing "Sunrise, Sunset,"
and her camp plans prove
she never wants to play music
together again.
I'm okay, I lie.
I'm still a twin,
just a
solitary
one.

He takes my hand.
I may not be your twin, he says.
But you're not alone.

Chaya
Crowded

Anisa and I scoot to make room
for Bailey, Parker, Jordan.
Before, I never thought I needed more friends—
Maya and Anisa were enough.
But now I find I like the table crowded.
I changed everything
because I love my sister,
because I thought it would make her happy.
But now it's making me happy, too.

Hey Chaya, says Jack—cute, tall,
tilting his head so his dark wavy hair
falls away from his eyes.
Hey. I wave back, stunned
he even knows my name,
the eighth-grade superstar, the lead in *Fiddler*.
He plays three instruments—guitar, drums, and piano—
not that I'm counting.
> *OMG Chaya, that was Jack Belcastro!* Anisa gushes.
I nod dumbly.
I hear he's applied to Carmody, Bailey says.

If he doesn't get in, I don't know who would.
What's that? I ask.
And Bailey tells me all about
the performing arts high school in Boston,
with normal high school subjects,
plus classes in performance
in an area of concentration—music, theater, dance.
And I think of Maya,
how we'd love a school
that focuses on music.

Maya
Away

At the lunch table with Jay,
I see a vision
of Chaya and me, away
at a beautiful boarding school,
playing piano,
studying,
in our dorm room
with twin beds.
Away,
she could return to who she used to be.
Away,
we could start over.
We wouldn't have to worry
about Mom's need to control us,
Dad's need for adventure,
Neel's constant chatter.
We'd miss them, but
Away,
we might be happier.

Chaya
Unmatched Set

You doing theater over the summer? Parker asks.

I signed up at Camp Allegro, I say.

I signed up again, too! Anisa says. We bump fists.

I hope we do Long Lost, I say. *It's my favorite musical, ever.*

Totally! Jordan says.

"All my life, I've been wondering why the world seeks to defeat me,"
Bailey sings.

"All my life, I've been searching for the one who completes me,"
I sing back.

The table joins in, loud and raucous,

and kids from other tables sing along.

But Maya stands abruptly

leaves the room

before we finish.

Now we're

an unmatched set.

Maya
The Plan

When Chaya and I get on the bus,
she leans toward me like she hasn't in months,
and tells me about Carmody,
the performing arts school
where her theater friends want to go.
I can see myself
at school there with Chaya:
she's surrounded by friends,
I'm alone.

I talk to Jay,
scour websites about boarding schools,
try to plan
the perfect moment
to tell her what I want us to do.

Chaya
Silent

We cheer on the last bus ride home of the year.
I did it.
Good grades, new friends, new ways
to make music.
I transformed myself
into someone different,
no longer a shadow,
a dark reflection
who pulls her sister down.
I found a Chaya who's separate
from her twin.

                        And Maya's been happier, too.

Right?

                        She was first in the class again,
                        straight As on everything,
                        the official pianist
                        for wind ensemble next year.
                        But she doesn't cheer.
                        Maya's silent
                        the whole ride home.

Maya
Schools

We go in the house,
drop our bags of papers and artwork,
shed the remnants of the school year.
Mom and Dad aren't home yet,
Neel's at a friend's house.
What's on your mind? Chaya asks.

> *Abby's touring boarding schools*
> *in the fall,* I say.
> *Don't you think we should, too?*

She blinks. *Why would we?*

> *So we can figure out where to apply*
> *next year.*

She gapes at me.
I either want to go to Carmody
or Atherton High.
They're both awesome,
and both free.
Why would you want
a stuffy boarding school?

> I shake out my ponytail.
> *They're some of the best schools*
> *around.*

So's Atherton. So's Carmody.
Where all our friends will be.

                Not all our friends. Abby—

Is barely your friend.

                And Jay—

Jay can follow Arvind's footsteps,
but we don't have to.
Besides, Mom and Dad
would never let us.

                Vimala Auntie can help convince
                Mom, I say.
                And some of these schools
                have amazing music programs.

Chaya scowls. *No way.*

                But I'm not letting go.

Chaya
Point and Counterpoint

A storm's rising,

      and this time it's from me.

Maya, don't let other people tell you
what you should be doing.

         No one's telling me anything.

         I think we should do this.

         Both of us, together.

I cross my arms. *I don't agree.*

         Maya crosses her arms, too.

         You think you know everything.

         No one can tell you anything!

What does that mean?

         You do whatever you want.

         You don't care about working hard,

         just take the easy way out.

Lightning zaps across my chest.

Easy? This year was scary, but
I'm happier than I'd ever be
if I just kept shuffling after you.
You're the one who always plays it safe.

         Maya's eyes go round.

I struggle with complicated music,
orchestral music,
while you play your simple chords and sing.
I'm still trying to get the best grades,
while you don't care.
Who's playing it safe?

My voice is full of thunder.
Try living my life for a week—even a few days.
You'd see how hard it is to reinvent yourself,
to try things you don't know that you're good at.
You'd be begging to go back to your old life
with Beethoven and Bach.

Maya shouts:
Stop thinking about yourself
for just a minute and try being me!

It'd be so easy to go back
to all that.
It made me miserable, I say.

You weren't miserable, Maya says.
But her voice rises at the end,
like she's asking a question.
Just look at boarding schools, she pleads.

I shake my head.
And live away
from Mom and Dad and Neel
and all our friends?

No way.

Well, I'm not applying to Carmody.

Silence stretches between us.

Then I have an idea.

We leave for camp in two weeks, I say.

I can't wait

for six weeks of green woods cold lake

music everywhere.

You think it's easy to be me?

Then prove it.

How? she asks.

Let's make a bet.

Maya
It's Time

Chaya's dared me
to switch places for the summer.
She'll be the classical piano player,
and I'll sing and play and act.
Whoever lasts the longest without being caught
gets to decide for us:
boarding school or Carmody.
We'll present a united front to Mom and Dad.
Easy for her—she's played classical piano,
while I've never set foot on a stage to sing
with everyone looking only at me.

I can't do it.

I know I'll fail,
and she knows it, too.
I should just tell her no.
But when I open my mouth,
what comes out is:
You're on.

I'm so pleased at the look
on Chaya's face.
She acts like she knows
what I'm going to say
before I even know it.
And she's usually right.

But not this time.
This time,
she thinks I'll make it easy for her,
but I won't.
I'm scared,
but I won't show her.
Not this time.

Because it occurs to me
of all the bad things that have happened
since I broke the mirror,
losing my sister
is the worst.
And now, it's time
to win her back.

Chaya
Goodbyes

We spend the two weeks between the end of school
and the beginning of camp saying goodbye.
I'll miss scanning tree branches for Neel,
watching him kick spindly legs in a pool,
snuggling under blankets as we watch cartoons.

Dad jokes and laughs,
filling all the space in any room he's in.
We spend weekends playing mini golf,
evenings grilling with friends.

Mom prepares our favorite meals,
sews labels in our clothes.
Her eyes shine as she looks at us,
smooths our hair.
She even runs her hand
over the pink streak in mine.
She takes our chins in her hands, squeezes gently,
then kisses her fingers.

My gems, she says. *I will miss you.*
We'll miss you, too, Mom, says Maya.

I nod. *But six weeks will fly by.*

Mom's smile is wistful.
Have fun, play music,
and it will be worth it.

I can't wait to throw myself
into all the stuff I've signed up for
and let Maya have her own fun
with Chopin and Haydn.
And maybe she'll play Debussy,
even if I won't join her.

Maya hasn't said a word
about our bet—
I bet she can't go
through with it.

Maya
Real

The night before we leave for camp,
I open Chaya's nightstand drawer,
pull out the bottle of pink hair dye,
go to the bathroom,
emerge with a streak that looks exactly like hers.
I hold out a bottle to her.
What's that? she asks.

> *Mom's hair dye*, I say.
> *We've got to fix yours now.*

I smile at the shock on her face.
Because this bet has gone from *maybe*
to *real*.

I'm not losing my sister
without a fight.
Not even if she's the one
I must vanquish.

Part Three
MIRROR TO MIRROR

Maya
Impostor

We barely speak on the three-hour drive to camp,
on highways and small roads and dirt paths
from Massachusetts to Maine.
Sunshine surrounds us,
and the leaves are lush and green
as we speed toward our home
for the summer.

No one notices that Chaya and I
aren't who we really are.
They're fooled by our hair,
and we're both keeping quiet.
Our parents are in their own world
in the front,
Mom gripping the door handle
while Dad drives too fast and hangs his arm
out the window.
And Neel's watching a video
laughing and commenting
to himself.

I'm glad I get to hide
with my earbuds in,
listening to music
that I forget
I shouldn't be listening to
Mozart,
Bach,
Pachelbel,
Debussy.
But when Neel catches me
moving my fingers
like I'm at the piano,
I stop,
start to sweat,
change the playlist
to Chaya's.

I make myself close my eyes,
nod my head
like she does.
I don't sing out loud,
but I find to my surprise
I like it.

Chaya
Arrival

It's a hot day for Maine.
The midday sun beats on my newly all-black hair
as we emerge onto the gravel
of the Camp Allegro parking lot.
I ignore the sweat dripping down my back
because we are *here*—
at camp,
my second favorite place in the world.
Birds chirp, mosquitos hum, leaves rustle
as we reach the central clubhouse,
where counselors greet campers and parents.
We find Dahlia, our favorite counselor,
who says hi and hands us folders
with cabin assignments and schedules.
I, "Maya," will be in Cornflower Cabin with no one I know.
Maya, as me, will be in Chrysanthemum Cabin with Anisa
and some other friends.
I grab Maya's arm, whisper to her.
You asked to be in a separate cabin?

                            Maya nods. *Figured it would be easier.*

The heat presses on me.

Maya decided she'd rather be alone
than with me and our friend.
Now I'm the one who'll be alone.
I couldn't wait
to be cabinmates with Anisa again
to join her for the first time
in the musical and rock band.
I glance at Maya's schedule,
now my schedule:
piano lessons, music theory, wind ensemble,
two different chamber groups.
How in the world does she cram all this
into every week?
I make a mental note to ask
about changing a few things.

Maya stares dully
at her schedule.
She sees:
pop composition, voice lessons, rock band,
and a huge block
of musical theater.
I know she won't last long
with that schedule.
She's going to quit
within the first couple of weeks,

and then I'll win the bet
and say we should switch back.

And then I can return
to the summer I've been waiting for.

Maya
Unfamiliar

We arrive at camp,
our second home,
where we've been coming every summer
since we were barely older than Neel.
I think back to that first year:
excited, nervous,
I'd never been away from home
for more than a single night's sleepover.
I clung to Chaya,
let her enthusiasm carry me
like our own secret song,
and I felt safe.
That summer,
at nine years old,
I found that
music was the most important thing
in my life:
a friend I could count on,
a tether to my twin,
a distraction from all
the bad things that could happen.

But now I look at ~~Chaya's~~
my schedule
and instead of coming home,
I see camp's been transformed
into something very
unfamiliar.
Just like Chaya.

And I have to live it.

Chaya
Cabin

I

walk with Mom

to Cornflower Cabin. It

won't be the same without

Anisa, without Maya. I meet the

counselor and junior counselor, nice

enough, but strangers. I glance at wood walls,

wood floor, wood ceiling, wood shelves glowing dimly

in the heat of the Maine summer. I make my choice of a bunk:

a top one, of course. Mom stares at me in surprise. She's right. Maya

always calls dibs on the bottom bunk. Has she already caught on to who

I really am? *Haha*, I say and quickly move my bag down. We

carefully fold my clothes, arrange them on shelves. Mom helps

me make the bed, and I fuss a bit about making it perfect, like

Maya would. Just like that, I'm moved in. There are two other

made beds, but no girls to go with them. I feel so alone already.

I miss Maya but can't let her win, can't let her switch be better

than mine. I must win this bet, must make my home in this

dim cabin reeking of bug spray and mustiness, must sleep here

among strangers, must make the whole world believe I am my

sister, must not panic. But in this cabin that doesn't feel like home

it will be hard, hard to remember who I am, to remember why

I'm here. We leave the cabin, step out into the punishing light.

Maya
Move In

We arrive at Chrysanthemum Cabin,
meet my counselors.
Dad, Neel, and I bring in
my bag
pillow
sheets.
I inhale the smells sounds sights
of my new home
for six weeks.
Wood walls
wood floors
wood bunk beds.
Posters
pictures
photos.
Instruments
intrigue.
The smell of adventure
with a hint of
homesickness.
Hey, Charming, comes a voice.

I look over and remember to grin at Anisa.

I saved you the top bunk, she says.

I hate the top bunk. It makes me feel like

I could

    tumble out

        at any moment.

I want to stay connected with the ground.

But I'm Chaya here,

who loves to sleep up high,

near the ceiling.

She's clearly related to Neel.

                Thanks, Anazing, I say.

                It sticks on my tongue.

                I hope Anisa didn't notice.

I swallow my discomfort,

start unpacking.

Neel grows bored in two minutes,

and Dad takes him outside.

So I organize my clothes myself,

make sure to fold them just a little

irregularly

which sets my teeth on edge,

but is perfectly Chaya.

Anisa helps me make my bed,

standing on the ladder to tuck in the sheets.

I can't wait for the musical, she says.

My chest grows tight.
Same! I say brightly.

But inside, I wonder
how in the world
will I bring myself to speak,
to sing, onstage?
And how in the world
will I fool Chaya's best friend
for the whole summer?

Chaya
By the Lake

When we're done unpacking,
Mom and I walk by the lake—
a small lake,
but it looks huge from here,
with bluish-green water that stretches far into the distance,
the other shore marked by tiny pines.
We stroll between the lake and woods
past cabins, practice huts
the dock.
Excitement and nerves teeter
back and forth
inside me,
and I glance at my wrist
to make sure my birthmark's still hidden.
Mom takes a tissue,
blots sweat from her face.

Paradise, she says.

We love it here, I say.
No cell service, no Wi-Fi,
just water and woods
and music.

Mom smiles. *This camp is special.*
I worry about you being homesick,
but I know you have each other.

I swallow, nod.
I do get homesick sometimes,
but because Maya's here,
I always have a piece of home
with me.
At least,
I used to.

I want to ask you something, kanna.

I wait for a speech
about washing my clothes
working hard
not getting into trouble.
(Not that Maya would ever
get into trouble.)

Take care of your sister.
I've been worried about her.

You're worried about Chaya?
When Maya's the one
who worries
who frets
who panics?

Mom looks at me for a long moment.
I fear she's seen through my pretense

and brace myself for all her questions.

Yes, says Mom. *Chaya's had a difficult year,*
changing her music and her friends
and her hair, of course.
She's been . . . unstable.

Have I really fooled her?
I think . . . it's made her happy, I say.

Mom looks at me, purses her lips.
Be good to your sister, kanna.
Watch out for her.
I think you've grown apart this year.
It happens sometimes.
You're getting older. I know you don't tell
us everything.
But whatever you're doing—

She pauses, and I know for sure I've been discovered
before camp even really starts—

Whatever you're doing, she continues,
make sure you're good to your sister
and yourself.
Promise me you'll tell us
about the important things.

I promise, I say softly.
But Mom . . .

Yes? Mom says.
Her face is open, inviting me

to share secrets.

I want to tell her
about Maya's anxiety
her panic attacks
her need for help. But
I now know
that's not my story to tell.

*You should take care
of yourself, too*, I say.

Mom smiles wearily. *We'll be fine.*

We walk to the end of the beach
then turn back.
I can't believe I've fooled her.

Mom puts her arm around me
as we reach the cabin.

I lean into her,
rest my head on her shoulder.
I'm just about her height now.
Soon, Maya and I will be taller than her.
Sometimes I miss being little,
when things felt simpler.
We still have our arms around each other
when we arrive at Chrysanthemum Cabin,
where Dad and Neel and Maya are waiting.

And she looks terrified.

Maya
Hurt

When I'm finished unpacking
Anisa and I go outside
to find Dad and Neel.

I want to see that tree, says Neel,
pointing at a towering red maple that rivals ours at home.

Anisa, can you go with him for a moment? Dad asks.
I need to talk to Chaya.

Neel, looking only—no climbing.
Anisa follows Neel into the woods.
Dad puts a hand on my shoulder.

Chaya, I hope you have a wonderful summer, he says.

                    Thanks, Dad.

I want you to watch out for your sister.

                    I always do.

I know something's come between you this year,
and I think it hurt her.

                    I stay silent,
                    because it's true.

But I think she hurt you, too.

                    What? I think.

I think she's been keeping a secret.

From all of us.

                  Does he know about the mirror?

I need you to find out what it is.
I need you to help her.
It may be
you're the only one who can.

                  I nod, silent still.
                  Does he know he's talking to me,
                  not Chaya?
                  Is this a trick?

But he says nothing else
as Chaya and Mom join us,
though a look passes between him and Mom.
We say goodbye
and I start my role as Chaya
for real.

Chaya
The Trumpeter

I switch out of one chamber ensemble
into a jazz ensemble
just for a change from classical music.
I arrive a little late to the first meeting,
open the door
to rough walls with music posters,
light streaming through big windows,
and four musicians, waiting for me.
A trumpet's smoky sound
drifts through the air.
I know that trumpet. Seriously?

> *Hey Maya,* Jay says.

> *Does this mean you're finally trying jazz?*

I want to turn around
run out the door
switch back to a chamber ensemble
sign up for opera lessons
take up the bassoon,
anything
to avoid being with Jay
for practice three times a week.

But then I see his easy smile,
his hand still raised in greeting,
and I know I can't do that,
or he'll know I'm not Maya.
She'd be excited to play music with him.
I grit my teeth,
force myself forward.

Jay introduces
our instructor, John, a jazz pianist
a cool drummer named André
Philip—a tall kid playing stand-up bass.
I say I've never played jazz before (the truth)
Jay says I'm an incredible pianist,
who'll pick things up fast (not the truth).
John invites me to listen first,
so I nod and take a seat.

John starts playing chords:
mellow yet intense,
familiar yet interesting.
Drums come in,
provide a structure
I hadn't noticed before.
Bass starts up,

adds texture, dimension.
Then Jay comes in
with a mute on his trumpet
that makes it softer,
like he's playing it   from far away.
When he solos, he plays notes
that are surprising,
surprisingly perfect.
I don't want them to stop.
But then the last notes fade
and I stand.
That was incredible. How do I start? I ask.
Jay lowers his trumpet and grins.

Maya
Musical

After breakfast and Whole Camp Meeting,
the campers break off and go to our first activities.
We don't call them classes,
but that's what they are.
I move my fingers surreptitiously,
longing to play chords that reverberate through me like home,
melodies and harmonies and accents.
But instead I find myself walking with Anisa
to Carnegie, the largest building at camp,
to learn about
the musical.
Anisa chatters as we go.
I wonder which show they chose?
Are you auditioning for a main role?
You were so great in Fiddler *this year.*

                              Thanks, I say, my insides freezing.
                              We'll see.

We arrive at the building,
where kids mill around in anticipation.
Campers, says Ella, the director, *are you ready to find out*
what we'll perform in six short weeks?

Everyone cheers.
I'll find some tiny part to play,
or better, stay backstage.
And then she tells us
it's a musical
about twin sisters separated at birth,
who find themselves reunited years later
at summer camp.
And just like that,
my face is burning,
stomach churning,
heart yearning.
Of all the musicals to choose!
Long Lost!

Ella explains the roles,
hands out audition sheets and tech information.
She plays music from the show.
It has complex rhythms, soaring melodies,
just like I remember.
"Matched Set" plays,
and my chest squeezes
from missing Chaya.

Chaya
An Unexpected Turn

At lunch, Anisa gushes
about the musical.
I can't believe they're putting on *Long Lost*
and I won't get to be part of it!
I want to march Maya outside,
tell her we need to switch back,
that I can't miss out on being in ~~my~~
our favorite musical,
that I'll do whatever she wants
in the fall.
I get to my feet and
freeze.
What's up, Maya? Jay asks. *Forget something?*
I stare at Maya.
                    She raises her eyebrows just like me.
But then I remember it's Maya.
                    She's not going to last a week.
Never mind, I say and sit back down.

Maya
Sloppy Joes

I take a small bite of sloppy joe,
put it down on my plate.
Then another bite.
I'm being careful with the messy food
because I don't want to stain Chaya's favorite tee:
a bird made out of music notes with
"Music takes flight in our hearts."

                    Aren't you hungry? Anisa asks.
A chill quivers at the back of my neck.
I can't lose our bet
over a sloppy joe!
I take a huge bite
drop a spot of sauce
right over the *e* in *hearts*,
and Chaya's eyes get huge.
Then she covers her mouth with her hand,
just like I do.

She starts chowing down.
You okay, Maya? Jay asks.
He glances at her left wrist,

where concealer covers her
birthmark.
He's onto her!
She stops
and takes a careful bite
of sloppy sandwich.

Chaya
Singalong

What part are you trying out for, Chaya? I ask.

> Maya grins. *I'm going to go for a lead.*
> *One of the twins, for sure.*
> *Too bad you're not into theater—*
> *it would be fun for us to play them both.*

Oh, she's good!
I blink my eyes innocently.
I could never imagine singing onstage.

> *I'm trying for a lead, too,* Anisa says.
> *It would be fun to play opposite Chaya.*

Jealousy flares,
and I drop my half-eaten sandwich
on the plate.
We're going to jam in our jazz ensemble, Maya,
Jay says with a greasy grin.
So glad you switched out of your chamber group.
What have I gotten myself into?
What I really want
is to be onstage singing all the *Long Lost* songs.
I sip my lemonade. It's just the first day of camp,
and I'm miserable.

Then Maya pipes up.
All-Camp Meeting was fun,
but we didn't sing our favorite song, she says.
Wherever we go, our hearts will
remember . . .

Anisa sings,
That special place for music,
that we will love forever,
Allegro, Allegro, beloved Camp Allegro,
Jay sings in a surprisingly nice tenor.
Then everyone else at our long table follows:
Allegro, Allegro, beloved Camp Allegro!

Maya leads the second verse,
and this time the whole cafeteria joins in.
Our camp song, the song that holds
almost as many memories
as *Long Lost*. Almost.

Maya has her head thrown back
in joy.
She's doing a better job being me
than me.
I can't tell if I'm impressed
or furious.

Maya
What Would Chaya Do?

I ask myself every day.
I audition for a lead
because I'm Chaya.
I move with Chaya's confidence,
speak with her bravado.
I think of how she convinced us all
she belonged in the world of *Fiddler*.
I'm Chaya,
reciting lines onstage
of a sister who misses the twin
she never knew,
a twin who discovers the sister
she's been waiting for
all her life.
And auditions
are surprisingly
easy
because I'm Chaya.
Because I know what it's like
to miss your twin.

Chaya
Improvisation

In jazz ensemble
I can play chords that don't sound terrible,
but I'm still scared to improvise.
What if I mess up and give away
that I'm not Maya, the more talented twin?
I linger with Jay after practice one day.

> *How do you know what to play when you solo?* I ask.

You know, improvisation
isn't just for jazz, he says.
Mozart was a famous improviser.
He had sections of compositions
that just said, "make up something here."
He loved improvisation, and taught
his students to love it, too.

> I raise an eyebrow.
> *NOW you reveal*
> *that you're a Mozart expert?*

Jay laughs. *I'm not an expert at anything.*
I didn't try solos until I'd been playing jazz
for a while.
But you're so amazing on piano,

so musical,
you'll catch on much faster.
No pressure, though.

I smile back at him.

Tell me how to start.

First thing to know, he says,
it's much easier on the trumpet,
because it's just one note at a time.

I don't believe that, I say.

Where did the arrogant boy go?
Who is this guy who's humble . . .
and kind of charming?

It's true. He wags his eyebrows.

Over time, you get a feel for it. Go for it.

There's that grin again.

Okay. I play a few chords from our piece.

Keep playing those with your left hand, says Jay.

and with your right hand . . .

Make something up?

Exactly.

Let's take it from the top, I say.

We start.

Jay plays a solo
completely different
from what he played during practice.

I'm still pressing chords,

can't bring myself
to make something up.
My heart pounds,
hands sweat.
I'm not ready, I say.
That's okay, says Jay.
It takes time.
He pauses, leans toward me.
You know nothing bad's
going to happen, right?
Not because of this.
He looks me straight in the eyes.
        I blink and nod
        like I know what he's talking about.
Has Maya shared something with Jay
that she never shared with me?

Maya
Fool Me

When we were little, Chaya and I
would switch places all the time
and fool the whole world.
We played so many tricks!
During games of hide-and-seek,
confusing everyone
about who was actually
It.
Talking on the phone to our cousins in California,
even once in India,
fooling our uncles and aunties,
until Mom found out and scolded us,
told us to have more respect.
But our pati laughed and patted our hands,
said she loved our cleverness.
And we were glad to see a smile
on her face so lined with worry.

We confused Jay so often
that he made a point
of memorizing our features,

listening to every nuance of our voices,
until he could tell us apart by sight or sound alone,
not needing to check the tiny birthmark on Chaya's wrist.

This year at camp
I'm avoiding Jay
and sticking with Anisa.
But I can't help my disappointment
that he hasn't noticed
we've switched.

Chaya
What Maya Would Want

I've spent the first days
in piano lessons with my teacher Lila
dabbling
in Bach and Mozart and Scarlatti,
practicing sight-reading and technique
and short pieces.
I haven't yet decided my piece
for the end of camp concert.
Lila suggests Chopin,
and the big bold sound is appealing,
but my hand aches just imagining
stretching, reaching for octaves.
I consider my options,
and I need to choose now,
because Maya would choose something
fabulous,
would jump at the chance to show off her skills,
would demand perfection of herself.
But what can I pull off
in a Maya-like way?
I get an inkling

of what it's like to be Maya,
to have the world expect so much of you
to expect so much of yourself.
My hands tremble.
If I'm pretending to be Maya,
I want to be Maya at her best.
Then I remember what we were supposed
to play this spring.
How about Debussy? I ask. *Not "Clair de Lune," though.*
There's a piece that sounds like flying.

                          Lila smiles,
                          hunts through a stack of music,
                          pulls something out,
                          starts to play.
An arpeggio starts in the left hand
                          continues to the right.

Up and down,
fluid and flowing.
An Impressionist painting,
Monet in music.
I think of our maple,
of twins who fly.

                          Lila finishes with a soft, strong chord.
                          That's Arabesque no. 1, she says.
I've found what Maya would want.
Perfect, I say.

Now I have to hope I can play it
perfectly.

Maya
Breathing Lessons

Who knew voice lessons
were all about
breathing?
I find myself
taking deep belly breaths
at every lesson
before I sing a single note.
You've got to strengthen your diaphragm
in order to project
and not hurt your throat,
says my teacher.
We spend almost as much time on posture,
breathing,
strengthening,
as we do on singing.
And once again,
I'm surprised
that I like what I'm doing as Chaya.
I don't feel the need
to press my palm.

Maybe because I don't expect to be
perfect.
Maybe
because I spend so much time
focusing on my breath,
I never forget
to breathe.

Back at our cabin,
when I tell Anisa
that I like breathing lessons,
she says, *Remind Maya*
it's helped me so much
with anxiety.
It might help her, too.
But talking to someone is even better.
Oh, I say.
So my sister has shared my problem
with her friend.
Anger sparks, but then I realize
Anisa understands
because she has it, too?

Chaya
Maya's World

I never noticed

how differently the world treats Maya.

At wind ensemble,
our conductor looks to me
to help keep the other kids on track.

At piano lessons,
Lila expects me
to play my piece perfectly
after just a couple of weeks,
so we can focus on fine-tuning
dynamics, emotion.

In jazz band,
the brilliant pianist
isn't brilliant at all.

Maya
Suspicion

Anisa and I walk from our cabin
to Carnegie, where we'll find out
our roles for the musical.
Any word from Jack? she asks.

        Jack who? I think. But I just shrug.

Anisa looks at me. *Wasn't he supposed to text you?*

        He didn't, I say. Did he?

        Chaya didn't tell me, either.

        Oh well, his loss.

Anisa's eyes drift to my pendant.
Isn't that . . . Maya's necklace? she asks.
She's onto me.

        Oh, yeah, we swapped, I lie.

        Because we knew we'd be in separate cabins.

Anisa frowns, still suspicious.

        Bet you can't beat me to Carnegie!

We take off into the leafy trees, and I've saved myself.
For now.
It's hard to keep fooling friends.
I just hope I don't get caught first.

Chaya
Not Good Enough

Arabesque no. 1, for all its flowing ease,
is challenging to play.
Despite hours of practice,
I can't get the rhythm,
can't feel how the parts operate
together.
Lila's patient, encouraging,
but I'm frustrated.
Why won't my fingers do
what my ears and brain and heart
demand?
Can I play this kind of music
anymore?

I still can't bring myself to solo in jazz,
afraid of playing something
that'll ruin the song.
I contribute nothing but chords
that anyone could play.
I can't even blame Jay
for psyching me out.

I'm failing.
Maya always makes music people remember.
I just want them to forget.

I'm not nearly good enough.
I wonder who will call my bluff?

Maya
Two Parts

I can't believe the cast list.
I
can't
don't
won't
believe it.
It's Chaya's dream come true,
my worst nightmare.
I've been cast as one of the leads,
one of the twins,
Hannah.
The other lead,
Anna,
will be played by Anisa.

How did I make myself get onstage?
How did I read those lines,
sing those notes
well enough to land this role?
I can't do it.
I know I can't.

I'm playing
two parts:
the role in the play,
and my role as Chaya,
pretending
to the whole world.

The world blurs around me
silence fills my ears
and I can't breathe.

Maya
Storm

Anisa's saying something,
her braces glinting
in the early evening sun.
I race from the room,
run into the woods.
I wish I could get lost,
never to be found.
It would be easier
than being onstage,
all eyes on me,
with no piano
to hide behind.
But the woods here aren't big enough.
Then I come across a huge red maple,
climb to a lofty branch,
and look down at the world below.
Feeling the strength of this maple
like our maple at home
brings me back to myself.
Neel is right.
Sometimes it's good to look at the world

from up high.

I remember the breathing
I've practiced during voice lessons.
I sit up straight,
expand my chest, my belly,
fall into the rhythm
of drawing air into my body
and letting it drift out again.
One-two-three-four-five-six-seven in
One-two-three-four-five-six-seven out
All my life, I've been wondering
why the world seeks to defeat me,
I sing.
And somehow,
I hear Chaya sing the next line:
All my life, I've been searching
for the one who completes me.
I sing the whole song,
Chaya's voice answering
in my head.

My stomach growls
I climb back down
to find Anisa at the bottom of the tree,
holding a plate.

Come on, she says.
I've got sandwiches.

We walk to the lake,
sit on the dock,
eat sandwiches and chips,
sip sodas.

I know what's wrong, Anisa says.

I know I'm done.
Chaya doesn't have panic attacks,
wouldn't run blindly from a stage.

You wish it were your twin
playing opposite you.

Yes, I say.
It's the truth.

She wishes it, too. I know it.
I know I'm not her, but we'll help
each other.

Maybe I'm not alone.
Maybe I never have been.

Chaya
The Race

It's Beach Day, the halfway point of camp.
We sit in the sun, float idly in the lake
and just before lunch is the big relay race
for the coveted Allegro Cup.
Each cabin has two kids competing,
from the youngest campers to teens.
Maya and Jay are Team Blue,
while I'm on Team Gold.
It's the first time Maya and I
have been on different teams
though we've been pulling
in different directions for a while.

The little kids start,
we cheer them on.
Each swimmer touches a buoy in the water,
then back to the next relayer.
The ten- and eleven-year-olds dive in,
and the crowd crescendos:
STAY TRUE, TEAM BLUE!
GO FOR THE GOLD!

It's almost my turn. I glance at Maya—
we're going to race each other.
She gets her tag and dives
with a head start in this race,
just like in life.
I lean over, tag my teammate's hand,
let momentum carry me
to dive into the freezing water.
My hands go numb
even as I kick and pull.
I head for the buoy bobbing ahead
as cheers float toward me.
Maya touches the buoy, starts back.
I've shortened her lead.
I touch the buoy, flip over,
put on a burst of speed,
lengthen my strokes pull pull pull
kick kick kick
ignore everything but my breath
and my sister swimming hard as she can
just a few feet away.
I've almost caught up,
legs tired, lungs burning,
arms numb but stretching,
barreling toward my teammate Connor's hand
as Maya races to Jay.

We tag at the same time.
Both boys dive,
and we collapse on the dock.

André drapes me with a towel
You kept us in the race! he says.
But Jay moves through the water
like his legs are a motor
and Connor can't keep up.
I take a step toward Maya, then stop.
She looks my way, and I can't tell
if she's inviting me closer
or telling me to stay away.
I'm chilled
in the strong summer sun
like I'm still in the water,
swimming toward nothing.
I'm so tired   of being apart.

Team Blue wins,
and I stay dripping, freezing
alone
as Maya and Anisa
celebrate.

Maya
Jamming and Creation

Rock band is easier than I thought.
I'm playing keyboard,
backing up our guitarist, bassist, drummer,
lead singer,
and I just have to play chords
and shake my head,
but I find myself singing backup, too.
If the spotlight's not on me, I'm fine.
We jam,
and I can hide.

I somehow make it through musical rehearsals
pretending to be Chaya.
Memorizing lines,
blocking,
choreography.
When I focus on those,
I forget to be terrified
about the audience that will be there
on performance night.

Composition is a different story.
I understand music theory,
know which notes should go with others,
but it's not that easy
to come up with novel melodies.
I keep comparing them to songs from the radio,
from *Long Lost* and *Fiddler on the Roof,*
and I'm defeated before I begin.

I have no idea how Chaya
reinvented herself this year.

Chaya
Campfire

At the Friday night campfire
I toast marshmallows next to Jay.
I like mine burnt,
but since I'm Maya,
I rotate my stick expertly,
not too close   not too far
to achieve the perfect level
of toasty gooeyness.
I pretend to have
the patience this takes.
Jay chats about our latest jazz band session
when I finally ventured a small solo—
terrible, but he talks about it
like it was genius.
Then he says his brother Arvind's been seeing live jazz
this summer in New York.
I smile and nod,
but my attention's on Maya and Anisa,
a few feet over, talking with their heads together.
My chest aches as I think of how much fun
they're having rehearsing for *Long Lost*.

Jay changes topics again.
Mom said in her last letter
we can visit Walden together,
if you like.
Chaya, too, of course.
Jay stares into the fire, and his eyes light up with gold.
Arvind has an alumni thing in the fall
and he could show us around.
I freeze.
The old Jay's back,
the one who convinced Maya to go away
from friends, parents, Neel.
From me.

>   *The fire's too hot,* I say.
>   I stand and walk into the darkness.

Maya
S'mores

I set my marshmallow on fire.
I'm making s'mores like Chaya
burnt on the outside,
gooey on the inside,
extra chocolate,
press firm,
bite.
Anisa's taking her time.
Chaya and Jay huddle across from us
smiling, laughing
about what?
Does he take her hand
like mine?
Does she tell him secrets
she won't tell me?
Chaya stands, and for a moment
I think she's coming over,
but instead
she stalks away.
It's almost August,
the mirror's curse almost broken,

and I've been worried about all the wrong things.
Chaya's healthy,
but I've lost her just the same.
Maybe not because of the mirror's curse,
but because of me,
my failings,
my imperfections.
It doesn't matter if seven years
are almost done.
The worst thing I can imagine
has already happened.
And it's all my fault.

Chaya
How Not to Say Goodbye

Camp is a whirlwind
the week before it ends.
I can't wait to see my family
and show off what we've learned,
but I don't want to leave
our camp family, either.

I stay alone after jazz band,
experimenting,
losing myself in melodies and chords,
my mind wandering,
fingers playing of their own accord.

It's lunchtime, so I stop
at Jay's cabin.
I call his name.   No answer.
I squint through the screen door. *Jay?*
He's on his bunk, hunched over,
crying.
I step back,
try to walk away.

I'm coming out, he says.

You don't have to—

         I could use some company.

         Let's take the long way to lunch.

I wait, and he comes out,
folds a piece of paper
and shoves it in his pocket.
He keeps his eyes straight ahead
as we walk to the lake.

         Mom sent me a letter with a photo

         from the last time

         we played mini golf at Pirate's Treasure

         before . . . you know.

He pulls out a photo
of ten-year-old Jay,
celebrating a hole-in-one
with Keerthi Uncle
with identical goofy grins.
Just out of the frame are Maya, Dad, and me.
We'd all celebrated, "triplets" and dads,
best friends.
Then just days later,
everything changed.
Oh, Jay, I'm so sorry.

         She sometimes springs stuff like this on me.

         I know she means well, but it's hard.

We keep walking.

> *My dad thought I was too scared*
> *of everything.*
> *He wanted me to try new things,*
> *be bold*
> *like him, like my brother,*
> *like your dad, like Chaya, like you.*

Like me?
But you're not scared of anything.
I think of how he dove into the water,
his fearless trumpet solos.

> *I'm scared of lots of things*, he says.
> *I just try anyway.*

But—

> *It's easy to take risks*
> *when you've already lost*
> *what's most important.*
> *If I channel my dad's courage,*
> *it's like I haven't said goodbye.*

I'm sorry, Jay. I didn't . . .
Know? Understand? Care?
Maya grew much closer to Jay after his dad died,
but I pulled away.
Did I really let petty jealousy
get in the way of our friendship?
All this time,

I've thought of Jay as a terrible person,
but maybe I'm the terrible one.

> He smiles sadly.
> *It's okay, Chaya.*

We've arrived at the cafeteria.
Did he just call me *Chaya*?
Have I lost the bet
so close to the end of camp?

I'm not sure I care.

Across the room Maya laughs,
the pink streak in her hair mocks me,
for even if I win this bet,
will we ever be close again?
Or will the wall I've put between us
stay?
Suddenly I know how it feels
when you've already lost
what's most important.

I wait for Jay to reveal our lies.
But he doesn't say a word.

Maya
Cold Feet

Chaya invites me outside to talk.
I tell Anisa I'll catch up with her later,
step into the sunshine
with my twin.
We walk together
through the shade of the woods
to the foot of the big red maple
I climbed weeks ago.
No helicopter seedpods now,
but I still think of our maple,
of twins that fly,
and how Chaya and I have flown
apart.

> *Let's tell everyone what we've done.*
> *We've been lying for too long,* she says.

I stare at her, my mouth agape.
Then realize
she thinks she's going to lose.
You have cold feet now? I ask.
A week away from our performances?
Too late. I don't care

if you're too scared
to pretend you're me anymore.
I'm going to win.
I know I started it,
but after all Chaya's done this year,
she doesn't get to change the rules
at the very end.
I leave her in the shadow of the tree.
I'm winning this bet
no matter what.

Chaya
Learn

Nothing's working out the way it should.
I thought this switch would be easy,
thought Maya would fold.
And now I've tried to apologize,
tried to get her to call off this bet,
tell the truth to our friends,
but she refuses.
I've learned so much about being Maya
this summer.
Has she learned anything
about being me?

Maya
Bargain

Are you okay? Anisa asks
on our way to rehearsal.

> *Yeah,* I lie. *I'm fine.*
> *Maya's just upset.*

I wish she'd talk to someone.
It helped me so much.
You can tell her it's okay.
It's no one else's business
for her to get the help she needs.

> I nod. I don't trust myself to speak.

We arrive at Carnegie
and all my lines fly
out of my head.
Lyrics, too.
You'd think I'd never learned these songs,
never rehearsed this play.
I'm going to fail,
and the worst disaster ever
will happen to my family,
I can feel it in my bones.
So to save them,

I make a bargain with the mirror:
I'll blunder through my performance,
then apply to boarding school,
get away from them all.
But I'll give up something, too.
I press my nail into my palm.
C C C C C C C

Chaya
Storm

I cling to my pendant,
shiver in my cabin,
lightning-lit,
thunder-shaken,
surrounded by sleeping campers
but very much alone.
What if? I ask myself.
What if I fail at the performance?
What if I fail at being Maya?
What if I never get her back?
What if I fail to protect her
like I always said I would?
There is no answer,
no *what-if* back,
just me
clinging to the pendant,
shivering in my cabin,
lightning-lit,
thunder-shaken,
alone.

Maya
Walk Away

I stand before the enormous tree—
it reaches to the sky
like I once reached my hands to Mom when I was little
asking
expecting
to be picked up and held.
The maple's leaves glow
where the sun shines through.
Tomorrow makes seven years.
I want so badly
not to be the curse-maker.
I want so badly
to keep my family safe.
For that,
I would do anything.
For that,
I'll give up music.
Forever.
I take out the charm.
The small silver *M* glints
in the late afternoon sun.

Chaya says I shine
when I play.
For her, I will hide that shine
bury my music
bury myself.
I dig a hole, place the bit of silver inside
walk away from what I love most.

Chaya
Twins Who Fly

Mom and Dad and Neel arrive with all the other families.
It's time for us to show
what we've learned this summer.
My hands tremble as I sit on the bench.
I want to make Maya proud,
not for the bet—
but because I love her,
and sometimes music can speak louder
than words.
I want to play beautifully,
not just *as* Maya,
but *for* Maya.

No need to hurry, says Mrs. Yu's voice in my head.
Take your time.
The audience can wait.
I pause a moment, center myself,
take a deep breath, blow it out,
put my hands on the keys.

The piece starts in the left hand

with gentle flowing triplets, smooth, hypnotic.
The right hand picks up, rises, falls,
I build to a crescendo, then fall away,
hands different
but in sync,
like me and my twin.
I close my eyes,
let my fingers go.
I've practiced so much
and they know the right notes
by heart.
Twins who fly,
our maple,
our home,
my sister.
Maya, who flies,
who doesn't need me
to help her stay aloft.
I finish with ascending arpeggios, and finally
a chord that's soft, yet strong,
just like my twin.
It wasn't perfect,
but it was my best.
The audience pauses
for just a moment
before the applause starts.

I hear Dad's whistle, Neel's whoops,
see Mom wipe her eyes.
I hope Maya knows I played
just for her.

Maya
Long Lost

I've spent six weeks pretending to be Chaya
pretending to be Hannah
in our favorite musical.
And it all comes down
to a single performance.
I wait for stage fright
to steal my breath.

But the overture plays,
and I don't feel like me,
Maya.
I'm caught up in a spell,
the illusion
that I'm Hannah,
separated from her twin,
lost and incomplete,
alone,
until she forms a connection
through letters
and music
and finds the sister

she didn't know she was missing.

I only hope
that after camp is over,
I can find my way back
to the sister
I know I'm missing.

Our performance isn't perfect,
but somehow a forgotten line,
a missed note,
doesn't matter as much
when you're onstage with friends,
all pulling in the same direction.
Anisa and I sing "Matched Set"
and I sing it for Chaya.

We finish the show
take our bows.
After this, I'm giving music up
forever
as I promised.
Does Chaya understand
what I tried to say tonight?
Has my music gone to places
words can't reach?

Chaya
Reunion

I'm in the audience with my parents,
holding Neel's hand as Maya comes out
dressed in my clothes,
the pink streak in her hair
lit up in the fluorescent lights.
She runs to me
like I'm the only one in existence.
She's the only one in mine.
She runs to me,
wraps me in a hug
like she'll never let go.
My twin,
who played the lead in *Long Lost*
better than I ever could.
You were stunning, I say.
Maya embraces Mom and Dad,
squeezes Neel and kisses his cheek.
She blinks, rubs her eye.
It's probably the mascara
she's not used to wearing.
Stage makeup's so dramatic.

Eyelash? I say.

I ask Mom for her compact.

    It's all right. Maya blinks.

Just take a look, I say,

and try to hand her the compact.

    No.

It'll just take a sec—

I reach out

but she pulls her hand back.

Maya
Crack

The compact crashes to the floor
a crack appears
in our perfect evening.

Chaya
Broken

Mom's compact falls
The mirror's cracked,
powder spilled.
Maya's face crumples
like we've lost a priceless heirloom.

and Maya's the one who shatters.

No, she says. *No, no, no!*

It's okay, I say. *Right, Mom?*

Of course, Mom says,
glancing between us in confusion.

But Maya starts to shake.

She'll give everything away.

I haul on her hand,
drag her out the door
to a shadowed spot outside.
What's going on? I ask.

But Maya has a closed-off
expression.
She's trapped inside her mind,
choosing misery
with happiness just in reach.

Maya! Tell me what's wrong!
It's the same refrain I've sung
for years.

> Maya shakes her head,
> mesmerized by the yellow light spilling
> from Carnegie, where we each just gave
> the performance of our lives.
> She starts to tremble.

You won the bet, I say.
We'll do whatever you like
for next year, for high school.

> Her shaking gets worse.
> The storm's coming on.

I have to reach her.
I think about the compact
crashing to the ground.
And ask, *Is this about the mirror?*

Maya
Truth

Surprise pushes away my fear.

You know about the mirror?

Chaya says,
I don't get why you're so upset.
It's completely replaceable.

She's right.

The only thing irreplaceable is her,

is us.

All this time, I've made myself feel alone.

But Chaya's always been right here.

So I tell her:

about the mirror,

the bad luck,

how it's all my fault.

How today marks

the end of seven years

how it all came crashing down

tonight.

Chaya
Seven

I can't believe
what Maya's said,
what Maya's felt
for seven years.
Seven years!
How could she keep this
from me?
She's been consumed with panic
from an old superstition?
I tell her
I'd smash all the mirrors in the world
if that would make her better.
I tell her
I thought I made her anxious,
I thought my shadow was pulling her down.
I tell her
I'm so glad she told the truth,
but she still really needs to talk
to Mom and Dad.

Maya replies, *Mom says we must
be perfect.*

And then we hear a cry.

Mom's voice is urgent.
Neel! she cries. *NEEL!*

Come back! Dad calls.

Maya grabs my arm

We run.

Maya
Mirror to Mirror

I recognize the worry
in my parents' voices.
It could be my voice
my worry
my panic.
The last time I broke a mirror,
Neel almost died.
What will happen now?
I must finally face
all that I've done.

Mirror to mirror,
so much has changed,
but it somehow feels the same.

Chaya
Nocturne

He was inconsolable, Mom says.
He said you're both lying
then ran off into the woods, says Dad.

Maya takes off through the open door.
I ask my parents to go to the clubhouse,
tell the counselor on duty,
who'll bring a team.
Dad nods.

Mom says, *We'll find Neel,*
and then we'll talk.
We have a lot to discuss.

Yes, I answer quickly.
Then I sprint.

The woods that seem so friendly, familiar
in the daytime
are different at night.
The bright half-moon is hidden
by thick foliage.
Creatures scurry in the undergrowth,

gossamer wings brush my face.

I trip and fall,

jump back up, keep running.

Where are you, Neel?

I follow Maya's voice

to the dock on the lake.

Maya's hunched over, panting.

Then she straightens, looks at the lake,

covers her face.

Neel wouldn't head for the water

at night.

If I say it out loud,

I can make it true.

Maya
Think

We race to cabins,
one by one.
No Neel.

Think, I say.
Where would he go?

He's mad, Chaya says.

We look up together.

We hurry to the maple tree,
almost as big as ours at home.
Neel, we know you're up there, Chaya calls.

No answer.

You need to come down.
Climbing at night's against
the rules, I say.

No answer.

Neel, if you don't come down right now,
Mom and Dad won't let you climb
the Eiffel Tower, Chaya says.

Just like I would.

No answer.

Chaya
Hold On

Five seconds
Ten seconds pass.

> *You're lying,* comes a small voice.
> *How come you two*
> *always tell me what to do*
> *then break the rules*
> *whenever you want?*

> *Hold on,* Maya calls.

We're coming up, I say.
We start climbing in the dark.

Maya
Lies and Reasons

We climb the tree in darkness
just like we told Neel
never to do.

                              Where are you? I call.
                    Here, Maya Akka, says Neel.
He knows my voice.
We never could fool him.

Neel's climbed higher in the dark
than he ever has before,
our little Hanuman boy.
I finally spy his small shadow
perched on a limb.
I scramble up,
get myself seated,
glad I can't see the ground below.

                         This is way higher than the
                         swing set at home, I say.
                    Why are you lying
                    to everyone?
                    Have you pretended to be

each other all summer?
he asks.

> *Yes,* I say. *But it was for a*
> *good reason.*

Neel crosses his arms,
and I warn him to put his hands back on the branch.
He shakes his head and scowls.

Chaya
Neither

It was a bet, I say.

                        Who won? Neel asks.

Neither, I say. *We both lost.*

                                  Maya stares at me in shock.

I can't believe you kept your secret for so long, I tell her.
That you told Jay, but not me.
That you wouldn't get help
when I couldn't help you.
You're not the only one
hurting.

Maya
We Can Go Together

The old arguments want to bubble up
but I stop them.
You're right, I tell Chaya.
Let's go down and talk some more.

> *One more minute*, Neel says,
> and we laugh.
> And so we stay there,
> together,
> like nothing can divide us.

Chaya
Crack

We start to make our way down
carefully,
me first, then Neel, then Maya.

Maya-Chaya-Neel! Mom calls.
Here in the tree! I reply. *We're coming down!*
We stop for a moment, each straddling the trunk,
our legs resting on the same limbs.
Then

Crack

A scream.

Maya
Pauses

There is music in the pauses
between notes.
There is life in the pauses
between moments
when you don't know
if anything
will ever be the same.

Chaya
The Fall

Something snaps,
we plummet to the ground,
something else snaps.
I can't catch my breath
until gradually I do.
I'm lying on my stomach
on something hard
with the weight of something else
pressing on me.

    Are you hurt? Mom's voice is near.
I feel a cool hand on my face,
turn my head.
I've never noticed how much Mom
looks like Maya when she's scared.
I move fingers and toes, check my head
for lumps and bumps.
I'm okay.

              Next to me, Neel moans,
              starts to shake.

Maya
Bleed

Something's poking at my hip.
I reach into my pocket,
gasp
at the sting,
pull
my finger away,
blood welling.

Neel groans.

Neel! I cry.

Is he bleeding?
Is something broken?

He can't speak! Shreedhar, call an ambulance!
Mom's voice is filled with dread.
But then, a small squeal.

Chaya
Hiccup

Neel? I say.

Are you . . . laughing?
Maya asks.

Neel hiccups, holds his stomach.

That was so much fun! he says
and stands.

Maya and I share a look
and I know what she's thinking.
Thank goodness he's okay.
And now, we want to kill him.

Maya
Switched

I press my stinging finger.
Nothing's broken
but my phone.

>*They were lying,* says Neel.
>*They switched places for the whole summer,*
>*and didn't tell anyone.*

Chaya
Consequences

Mom pats Neel's whole body.
Dad's hand reaches down, and I take it.
Chaya, he says.
I think you two have explaining to do.
He raises a brow,
but there's a twinkle in his eye.

> *I agree*, says Mom,
> glaring at us both
> as she helps Maya to her feet.

Maya
It's Time

I pat my hair.

Is the pink still there?

We know you switched places, Dad says.

We knew it the day we dropped you off, says Mom.

Dad nods. *We figured you were working something out
between you.*

Mom picks up Neel. *But now it's time to tell us why.*

Neel winds his arms
around Mom's neck.

Yeah! he says.

Chaya
Tremble

Maya grabs my hand.
We'll tell you everything, she says.
Let's go to the clubhouse.

She's trembling, breathing hard,
but I'm not sure it's panic.

Maya
Break

While everyone else

is at the dance in the cafeteria,

I hold

Chaya's hand

break

the silence

I've been

holding

for seven years.

I finally share

all I've been feeling

for so long.

How I tried to keep it

from everyone.

The broken mirror,

the seven years' bad luck,

the worries,

the panic,

the guilt.

The C C C C C C C into my palm.

How I tried not to fail,

and kept failing at it.

How Chaya tried to help,
but I wouldn't let her.

Chaya
Try

I tried to get her to tell, I tell my parents.
And when she wouldn't let me,
I tried to understand why.
I thought it was my fault.

Maya inhales sharply.

I turn to her.
I thought it was my fault,
that my success made you feel smaller.
So I changed what I looked like,
what I played.
I tried,
but it wasn't enough.

Maya
Blurry

The world is blurry
as I talk about our bet,
how pretending to be Chaya
gave me the courage
not to be perfect.
The world is blurry
as I face my parents and say,
I need help.

Mom takes my hand.
Yes, kanna. We'll get it.
All of us. She looks at Dad.
No mirror caused this.
I've seen the signs in you
because
I've seen them in your pati,
in myself.
I didn't let myself see
that you reflected me.
And now her face is blurry.

Dad takes my other hand.
Promise us
no more secrets.
I give a shaky nod
and Chaya smiles through tears.
And it's like
breathing clean air,
like hearing music
for the first time
again.

Chaya
Nothing Broken

Mom looks at me and says, *I'm sorry I didn't understand*
what you were trying to do.
I asked you to take care of your sister,
but not by yourself.
It's our job
to care for you all.

Still, says Dad,
nothing's broken that can't be mended:
not a tooth,
not a limb,
not a heart.

Maya
Not Perfect

Strong arms around me—
Chaya
   Neel
      Dad
            Mom.
                 My girl, she whispers, *I'm so sorry.*
                 I wish you'd told me.
                 My love isn't perfect
                 but you'll always have it.

Chaya
Brave

Maya thinks I'm the brave one.
But she's just done
the bravest thing of all.

Maya
What If

all the bad things
aren't my fault?
What if I don't have to be
alone?
What if becoming Chaya
has made me start to think
like Chaya?
What if that's a good thing?

Chaya
Chome On

Mom and Dad take Neel to their hotel.
Maya and I hold hands—
after so much time apart,
we won't be separated now.
We are starting toward the cabins
when Jay and Anisa find us.
Jay says, *Come with us.*

> *Connor's the DJ for the dance tonight,*
> Anisa says.

And you owe us an explanation, says Jay.

> *Oh*, Maya says.

Well, I say.

> *You know we knew*
> *what you'd done*, Anisa says.

You . . . did? I ask.

> *Chome on*, says Anisa.

We've both known you forever, says Jay.
Pink hair can't change that.

> So basically, all summer
> we've fooled exactly
> no one.

Maya
Freckle

What gave us away? I ask.

Sloppy joes, says Jay.

Yes, and breathing exercises, says Anisa.

Not remembering important conversations.
Jay shakes his head.

And the necklaces, Anisa adds.

But the final straw was

the freckle!

But I've been hiding it,
and Maya's been drawing hers on
for the entire summer, Chaya insists.

Oh, I say.

We share a look.

Swimming, we say in unison.

We're sorry, Chaya says.

Really sorry, I agree.

It's okay, Jay says.

We figured it was a bet, Anisa says.

So who won? Jay asks.

Chaya
The Winner

Maya and I share a look.

    Both of us, she says. *And we get to choose our prize.*

I want to share everything with you, I say.

    Me too, says my twin.

Later, there'll be more time to talk.

But my heart sings to be on the same side

again.

And the four of us go to the dance—

best friends and sisters.

All of us, together.

Maya
The Lake

On our drive home,
we stop by the lake, a spot
with a small hill,
a large rock,
a launching point.
Mom's already in the water, waiting.
Dad tosses Neel, then jumps in after.
Then Jay, with a high-pitched whoop,
Anisa next, a perfect cannonball.

Chaya
Maybe

Maybe I don't need to play the part
of Maya's protector.
Maybe I can be myself,
and go where my heart leads.

Maya
Leap

Summer sun sparkles on the lake.
I shiver on the mossy rock high above
the sound of water and wind fading
as I look down
to the faces of friends,
of family, beckoning.
Chaya steps beside me.
Bet I can make a bigger splash, I say.
She closes the distance
and we leap.
Sometimes falling feels like
flying.

Chaya
Coda

A bright August day,
clouds drift across an azure sky,
a beautiful day to climb
the Eiffel Tower.
Neel agrees to take the stairs,
not the scaffolding.
We are noisy as we climb,
chatting about music and theater
and dental jokes,
no more secrets between us.
We put away the silence
that hurt us.

Maya
Tutti

We get as far as we can by foot,
but the elevator to the very top
is out of service.

>   We look at Neel.
>   *At least we climbed*
>   *as high as we could*, he says.

We photograph Mom and Dad
in the same poses
as on their honeymoon.
Mom looks carefree,
and Dad just looks at her.
Then the photos of the kids:
alone,
in pairs,
all three.
Then all five of us, smushed in close,
at the top of the world.

We have more work to do
as a family,
but we've made a start.

Maya and Chaya
Encore

Our twin reflections are identical
almost.

People can tell us apart.

We have
wavy black hair,

pink streak or not,

big brown eyes,

bright and inviting,

the same height

for reaching,

the same voice

for singing,
for acting,
for sharing.

Our music flows straight
from our brave hearts.

No illusion or shadow,
we don't need protecting,
no secrets between us.
She's the one

I look up to,

the one I come home to,
the best part of me
in a separate space.
She's the one
who sees without showing
knows without telling
loves without asking.
We're a matched set,
not perfect,
not the same, but still
in sync.

Acknowledgments

The pandemic has been difficult for nearly everyone, my family included. Writing and revising this book while my family dealt with illness, anxiety, and death was a challenge I never expected, but I did it with the help of many wonderful people in my life.

Brent Taylor, my fantastic agent, encouraged me every step of the way, including and especially when things were difficult. He always helps me see the bright side of any publishing situation.

My brilliant editor, Alexandra Cooper, helped me take this story from a not-so-great first draft to the book it is now. I am so grateful for her incredible notes and subtle understanding. Thanks to Rosemary Brosnan's vision, Quill Tree Books brings vibrant, diverse voices to children's literature, and I'm thrilled to be one of their authors. Many thanks to the whole team at Quill Tree—including Allison Weintraub, assistant editor; Kathryn Silsand, senior production editor; and Alison Kerr Miller and Dan Janeck, proofreaders. I'm blown away by book designer David Curtis's ingenious cover and interior design, and artist Vrinda Zaveri once again stunned me with her gorgeous cover art.

I interviewed several sets of identical twin sisters for this book, and I was astounded by how close they were—so close that it was hard for me to truly comprehend. I'm indebted to Priya Sarin Gupta and Jaya Sarin Pradhan, Amitha Knight and Yamini Howe, and my wonderful mother-in-law, Christine LaRocca, and her twin, Marie Caronia, for giving me insight into twin relationships. I hope I did justice to them all.

My amazing friend and critique partner Theresa Milstein and I have many parallels in our lives that make us joke that we're "twins." Theresa read and reread so many revisions of this book that I can never express how much I owe her. Thank you, Theresa, for your friendship, patience, and writer's eye. You keep me laughing when I want to weep. My life is richer because you're in it.

As always, my husband, Lou, and my children, Joe and Mira, are the wellspring of joy that allows me to write. They are my daily reminder that together, we can weather even the most difficult times. I hope that this story helps readers feel the same way.